# Fatal Misunderstanding

# Fatal Misunderstanding

Darlene Duncan

First Paperback Edition © 2022 Darlene Duncan
ISBN:  978-0-9723324-8-4

Published by Ocean Breeze Publishing

This novel and its characters are a product of the author's imagination. Some locales may be factual but are used fictitiously.

To Charlotte, the love of my life,
my biggest fan and with
whom all things are possible.

# CHAPTER 1

A cottage in Cerridwen

Mirabel was a creature of habit. Her afternoon routine was to make a smoothie, put the blender jar to soak while she finished her drink, then head to her garden to tend her herbs and flowers.

The person watching from the edge of the woods knew this routine. She waited patiently, hoping for an opportunity to slip into the cottage.

This particular afternoon as Mirabel was adding smoothie ingredients to the blender, she heard her phone ringing. It was in the bedroom on her nightstand. For a second, she considered just letting the call go to voicemail, and then thought better of it.

It might be Sybil, asking me to work the dinner shift at The Cauldron.

As soon as Mirabel disappeared from view, the person watching from the edge of the woods moved quickly into the kitchen. They dumped the contents of a vial into the open blender, returned the empty vial to a pocket and ran back to the trailhead.

Mirabel returned to the kitchen as she finished her phone conversation. "All right, Sybil. I'll see you in the morning."

She put the phone on the counter and returned to making her smoothie.

"Well now, where was I? Ah yes, I think I still need to add the fresh mint." Mirabel dropped a couple of mint leaves into the blender. But before she could put the lid on and fire it up Sasha jumped up on the counter and got between Mirabel and the blender.

Mirabel smiled at the feline, scratched the top of the cat's head, and ran a hand down the long sleek body. She scooped the cat into her right arm, held her, and used the other hand to put the lid on the blender and start it.

Sasha head butted Mirabel's chin and meowed.

"Yes, I love you too, but you know you're not supposed to be on the kitchen counters."

She placed the cat on the floor and then turned off the blender. While she was pouring the smoothie into a glass, Sasha jumped up on the counter and pushed on the blender jar Mirabel was pouring from.

"What has gotten into you today? You nearly made me spill my smoothie." With a glass in one hand the blender jar in the other, Mirabel scowled at the cat, and in a very firm voice said, "Down! Now!"

Sasha looked up at her and Mirabel almost relented, instead she said, "You heard me. Down!" The cat hesitated. "Now!"

Mirabel's tone of voice told the cat she was in trouble. With feline grace, Sasha jumped to the kitchen island and sprang to the top of the pantry cabinets.

2

Shaking her head in disbelief Mirabel finished pouring her smoothie, set the blender jar down, and took a big gulp of the creamy concoction. She looked at the glass questioningly, then took another drink.

"A little on the minty side. Maybe I'd already added the mint before Sybil called. Oh well, good thing I like mint." Another large swallow of the smoothie almost emptied the glass.

She placed her glass on the kitchen island, put the blender jar in the sink and filled it with water. It would get washed when she washed her dinner dishes.

Sasha jumped down from the cabinets and knocked Mirabel's glass to the floor. The shattering of glass startled Mirabel, she spun around from the sink in time to see a streak of black heading back to the cabinet tops.

"Sasha, you bad girl. What's gotten into you?"

The black cat at the top of the pantry, well out of reach, looked down, and meowed.

Mirabel swept up the broken glass and mopped up the little bit of smoothie that had been in the glass when it hit the floor. Looking up at the cat, she said, "It's a good thing I'd almost finished that drink."

With a sigh she grabbed her gardening gloves and headed outside. She left the kitchen door open, letting the mild October air into the small house.

An hour later, she was dead heading the Marigolds when the first cramps hit her. They increased in severity and were followed by vomiting. By the time Mirabel headed for her phone to call someone for help, it was too late.

She reached for her phone on the kitchen counter as she doubled over in pain. Her hand slid off the counter, without her phone, as she sank to the floor.

# CHAPTER 2

Larissa Carpenter stood in the parking lot admiring the architecture of Ravenswood Manor, the bed and breakfast where she and her friends would be spending the weekend.

The two-story wood frame house was painted white with a black trim. The screened in porch gave the impression that it wrapped around the house completely. The second story offered a balcony that overlooked the parking area out front.

Harriet Walsh, Larissa's best friend, also stood next to the car, looking at the manor. She felt an energy that she recognized, coming from the building, and a faint smile touched her lips.

It was the power of what many call magic. To Harriet it was simply the energy of the beliefs of past and current residents. Having been born and raised in New Orleans, homes containing such energy were familiar to her.

The double doors set in the middle of the house were bracketed by two windows on each side. There were four steps leading from the gravel path to the landing for the screened in porch. At each end of the four steps were jack o'lanterns.

On both sides of the steps was a postage size grassy area. The one to the right had a blow-up witch and cauldron. The one to the left was occupied by a dragon that was at least ten feet tall.

The dragon was a metal sculpture that looked as if it was a permanent fixture.

Larissa stared at the dragon, thinking, "Wow! If I had room at my place, he'd look great in the entry way. Hell, I may have to buy a house that's suitable, just so I can get one of these."

"Is there some reason you want to stand out here and stare at the building?"

"I'm not staring at the building. I'm admiring that dragon." Larissa looked at Harriet and smiled. "Come on. Let's go inside."

Neither of them grabbed their weekend bag from the car. Larissa pushed the remote to lock the car and they walked to the house.

Larissa opened the screen door to the porch and ushered Harriet ahead of her. They stopped just inside the shade of the porch and checked out the padded rocking chairs. There were four on each side of the doorway to the house. None were in use.

The double front doors to the house were open, as was the wide back door at the end of the long hallway, creating a funnel for the cool October air to flow through the house.

The floor of the porch was lined with more carved pumpkins. Each one was unique; some were funny, and others were intended to be scary.

Larissa stepped inside and surveyed her surroundings. To her left was what she considered a living room. There was a couch, several chairs, end tables, and a fireplace. The fireplace was set, ready to be lit.

There were holiday themed decorations throughout the room but the two skulls on the fireplace mantel were what drew Larissa's attention. Even though the skulls were facing into the room, their eyeless sockets seemed to look right at you.

Her eyes swept across the wide entryway and down the hall, toward the open back door. On the left wall were two closed doors. Outside she could see a small section of a garden. As Larissa moved her eyes to the right coming back to the front of the house, there were two closed doors. Then there was the staircase. She couldn't tell if the space under the stairs was utilized or if it was wasted space.

An image of a young Harry Potter living under the stairs at his uncle's house came to mind and Larissa smiled.

At the foot of the stairs was an open door. From the sounds and smells emanating from that room, it was a kitchen. To her immediate right was a dining room. The distressed wood table would comfortably seat fifteen. The wall the dining room shared with the kitchen held a sideboard that was obviously used as a buffet.

"Welcome to Ravenswood Manor."

Not having heard anyone approach, Larissa was startled by the voice only a few feet away and she spun around to her left.

"I'm sorry. I didn't mean to frighten you." Standing in front of her was a smiling woman who appeared to be in her mid-thirties, dark hair framed her face, above her snub little nose were a pair of brown eyes with flecks of green. Her mouth was wide, and her lower lip was full.

"I'm Amanda Colton." She held Larissa's gaze. "You must be Ms. Carpenter. It's nice to meet you."

Amanda moved her eyes to Harriet. "And you must be Harriet Walsh. I've heard a great deal about your café and the delicious foods you prepare. I do hope our fare will meet with your approval."

Harriet returned her smile. "I'm surprised that word of My Place has reached this far from Coventry Beach."

Amanda tilted her head and her smile broadened. "Well, to be honest I go to the beach on occasion, and I've been to My Place."

Harriet laughed. "Yes, I recognize you, now. You order a mixed green salad, and the two ladies for dessert."

Amanda's smile faded and her complexion went pale. She looked like she had just seen a ghost. Her hands reached out for something to grab for support.

Larissa grabbed her hands and asked, "Are you alright?"

Harriet stepped closer to Amanda to offer her support.

Amanda drew in a couple of ragged breaths, forced a smile, and said, "Yes, I'm sorry. I don't know what came over me. I probably just need to drink more water." She pulled her hands from Larissa and took an unsteady step away from Harriet. "Thank you. I'm fine now."

Larissa started to say something but before she could speak, Amanda said, "Let's get you to your rooms. If you would like you can give your car keys to my daughter, Cassandra, and she'll get your bags."

Entering the dining room from the kitchen was a younger version of Amanda only with long blonde hair, instead of the bobbed brunette hairstyle of her mother. "Mother, you know Ms. Carpenter may not want a stranger in her car."

Without hesitation, Larissa tossed the key fob to Cassandra, and smiling said, "It's insured."

At the top of the stairs Amanda pointed to the room at the right end of the hallway and handing Larissa the key said, "That's your room." Directing Harriet's attention to the room next door to Larissa's she said, "That will be your room. Unless you would prefer one of the other rooms."

Smiling Harriet said, "I'm sure this room will be just fine. Thank you."

The door to Larissa's room was open, as was the door to the balcony outside her room. In the garden beyond she could see a Magnolia tree.

On each side of the doorway was a stuffed chair. At the foot of the king size bed was a bench.

Amanda said, "We like to open the rooms up for a good airing when the weathers like this. Unfortunately, this kind of weather never lasts for long around here." She sighed. "As soon as this cold front passes through we'll be back in the mid-eighties before you know it." She looked at Larissa. "If it's too cool for you, feel free to close the doors and adjust the thermostat."

Harriet looked at Larissa, "How many rooms did you reserve?"

Amanda looked from Larissa to Harriet and answered, "The entire second floor is reserved for your group" she paused "with the exception of Nicole and Minerva's room. It's the one at the end of the hall."

Before Larissa could voice a complaint, she continued, "She's my business partner. Right now, she and her daughter are out of town." She held Larissa's gaze. "They're due back on Wednesday, until then the second floor is yours. When are your expecting the rest of your party to arrive?"

Cassandra came up the stairs with their bags in hand. She walked past the adults into Larissa's room. Larissa started to tell her which bag was hers, when she saw the girl put the correct bag on the bench at the foot of the bed.

Turning back to Amanda she said, "I'm not sure. I'll look for them when I see them coming. However, I imagine they'll be here before dark."

"I'll leave the other room keys with you, and we'll leave you to get settled in." Cassandra came out of Harriet's room and she and her mother started down the stairs.

With the room keys in her hand Larissa turned toward her room thinking, "I wonder how long it will be before the entire town knows who I am. Maybe I should have held off using my real name and just paid cash for everything."

On the stairs Amanda stopped and looked in Larissa's direction. "Ms. Carpenter, no one will learn your identity from anyone here at Ravenswood."

Larissa held Amanda's gaze for a moment. She found it unnerving that it seemed as if the woman had read her thoughts. "Thank you."

# CHAPTER 3

Sara and Elizabeth arrived just after five. Tammy showed up shortly after five thirty.

Larissa greeted Tammy at the top of the stairs. "You have a choice. We can share a room, or you can have one of your own."

When Larissa first brought up this weekend getaway to Cerridwen, Tammy had been excited. It would be an opportunity to see people she hadn't seen in quite some time, one in particular. However, since late afternoon she'd felt uneasy.

Now she forced a smile and said, "Where's our room, love?"

Tammy closed the room door and pulled Larissa into her arms and delivered a kiss that was a promise of things to come. Their interlude was soon interrupted by Harriet in the hall.

"Come on you two. It's time for dinner."

Coming down the stairs, Larissa watched and listened to the three women waiting below. They were all introducing themselves to one another. Everyone knew Larissa and Tammy.

Harriet looked up at Tammy and Larissa and said, "LC, why didn't you tell me that you knew a CFP?" Turning back to Sara she said, "When you have a chance, I'd love to talk to you about planning for my future."

"Certainly. Let's get together with our calendars sometime this weekend."

"Definitely."

Amanda stepped out of the kitchen and walked to the group. "It will be quite dark by the time you head back." She handed each woman a pocket size flashlight and smiling added, "You'll be glad to have these."

Tammy's soft English accent added a hint of mystery to the already mysterious atmosphere at Ravenswood, as she said, "Thank you, Amanda."

Something about the way Tammy and Amanda looked at each other caused Larissa to think they knew each other. Not that they'd had a relationship, simply that they knew each other.

All the ladies thanked Amanda for her consideration as they headed out the door and toward the town.

It was a pleasant walk as the sun began to set, casting shadows from the large oaks that lined the road. There was no sidewalk. There was also no traffic.

Larissa was happy that none of them felt the need to talk. She had started wondering if she'd made a mistake inviting so many people

Their silence put Larissa's mind at ease. When she'd come downstairs to find Harriet, Beth, and Sara all chattering away, her first thought was, "My god, I hope they're not going to be yammering like that the whole time."

However, now that everyone was introduced the women were all silent during the walk to town. It seemed each one was enjoying the quiet sounds of nature that surrounded them.

The rustling of palm fronds in the breeze. The skittering of small animals in the underbrush and the calls of the birds.

It had occurred to her that perhaps she should have made it a weekend for two, just her and Tammy. But she was afraid that Tammy might take that as a signal their relationship was moving to another level. A level Larissa wasn't ready for, at least not with Tammy.

As they reached the edge of town, the two-lane street with no parking and sidewalks on each side, with glass storefronts set in wood buildings reminded Larissa of the streets from old westerns.

Yes, but these are concrete sidewalks and there's no place to tie up a horse. And then of course there are the Halloween themed decorations.

Ghosts and vampires hung from the wood shingled roofs that covered the sidewalks. Carved pumpkins bracketed the doorway of virtually every shop. Orange and purple LED lights were draped here and there. The street light globes were skulls with LED lights for eyes, ranging from purple to blue to red.

"These decorations are awesome. Especially, the streetlights." Then Larissa asked, "Does anyone know what kind of restaurants are available in Cerridwen?"

Sara and Beth spoke at the same time.

"No."

"No." Sara laughed softly. "I've meant to come here on several occasions, but something always seemed to get in the way. This is my first time here."

Harriet said, "Don't look at me. I've been too busy hiding from my stalker and running a business to have time to play tourist."

"What?" This was the first Beth had heard about Harriet's stalker. She looked at Sara, her expression demanding to know more.

Larissa said, "Not to worry, Beth. He's dead now."

"Oh." Beth was a shy withdrawn individual on a good day and Larissa watched her close down a bit more.

Larissa wanted everyone to have a good time and she looked at Sara. "Perhaps I should give her the details. It might make her more relaxed."

Sara shrugged and Larissa moved to walk next to Beth, while Sara moved up near Tammy and Harriet.

"Harriet was engaged to a man named Alan Henry. Prior to the engagement Alan was the perfect man, considerate and caring. Once they were engaged, he became controlling and demanding. After she broke off the engagement, he began stalking her. She took out a restraining order, which he repeatedly ignored. She moved to a new town. He followed her." Larissa paused and took a long breath. "She thought he'd lost her trail when she got to Coventry Beach. She was wrong. He drugged her and took her to a house he had rented. Fortunately, the police got to her in time."

"Got to her in time?"

"Yes, well, intentionally or accidentally, it turned out he had given her too much of the sedative he used to subdue her and if she hadn't been found when she was…she would have died of the overdose."

Larissa waited while Beth quietly processed everything she'd just been told.

"So, I suppose, the police shot him when they found where he had Harriet."

"No." Larissa sighed. "He wasn't at the house when they found her."

"So…"

"After Harriet left the hospital, she came to my house. He tried to get her from there and that's when he was shot and killed."

"By you?"

Larissa gave a soft laugh. "No, by FBI Special Agent Amber Hoffner."

It occurred to Larissa that she hadn't heard from Amber for quite some time. *I wonder how she's doing. I should contact her when I get back home.*

"Oh."

Larissa looked at Beth and could see her beginning to relax.

Beth looked at Larissa and said, "Thanks for telling me."

"You're welcome." Larissa looked at the rest of their party that was a good distance ahead of them. "What do you say we catch up with the others?"

Beth smiled. "Yeah."

Before they were within earshot of the others, Larissa said, "Do me a favor and let's drop this topic around Harriet. It's something she'd like to forget. If you want any more details, come ask me."

With a smile that just touched her lips, Beth responded, "You got it."

The window shopping had brought the group's progress to a crawl. When they rejoined the others, Larissa said, "Now what, if anything, has been decided about food?"

They all laughed.

"Ah yes, Frodo is among us again" Tammy said. "The best restaurant and unless things have changed since I last visited here, the only restaurant, is The Cauldron."

"Then The Cauldron it shall be."

# CHAPTER 4

The five women strolled down the main street of Cerridwen.
Window shopping, reading notices of upcoming events, and
talking among themselves as they moved toward The
Cauldron.

There was nothing to set them apart from the other tourists
in town beyond the fact that they were all women of a similar
age. Most of the tourists were either heterosexual couples or
families.

A family with three rowdy children was coming down the
sidewalk toward the women. Sara looked at the open sign on
the door to the Tarot reader's shop.

"Come on guys. Let's check this out." Before anyone could
voice an objection, Sara and Beth were inside the dimly lit
shop.

After Sara and Beth entered Tammy grabbed the door and
held it for the rest of the group, making her the last one in.
From the back of the group, she recognized Edgar, the shop
owner. Before he could say something that would give away
the fact that they knew each other, she shook her head. The
motion was barely perceptible, unless you were looking right
at her, as Edgar was doing. His eyes slid off her and took in
the rest of the group.

What's happened? I was looking forward to seeing people here. Why don't I want the others to know I know some of these people?

In the center of the room was a sectioned table, approximately six feet long. The legs were as big around as a man's thigh. Considering the weight of the table and its contents it was a good thing the legs were so strong. There were two levels of sections, and each section held a different type of crystal or rock. On the back wall to the right were shelves holding containers of dried herbs. In addition, some dried herbs hung from a string that ran behind the counter.

"Welcome ladies. I am Edgar The Enlightened. How may I serve you this evening?"

As his deep baritone voice caressed her ear, Harriet smiled and thought, "He's a little fellow for such a deep voice."

Harriet closed her eyes for a second, feeling the environment around her with all her other senses. When she opened her eyes, her gaze met Edgar's. There's an energy surrounding him. He has a true gift. She tilted her head a fraction. His gift scares him. Too bad.

The noisy family passing by outside caught Edgar's attention and he sighed. You didn't have to be psychic to figure out why the ladies had stepped into his shop.

Tammy knew Edgar was the real deal, but she had no desire to have her cards read or to know her future. In her mind, ignorance of the future was preferable to worrying about how to change something that may or may not be changeable.

In the silence that followed the departure of the noisy family, the growl from Larissa's stomach was audible. "Sorry guys but right now, food is my priority." She smiled at Edgar. "Perhaps we'll stop by later."

Edgar chuckled and bowed. "As you wish."

Since Tammy was the last one in, she was nearest the door which she held open for her friends.

Before leaving Harriet stepped up to Edgar, looked him in the eyes, and quietly said, "I'll see you later."

Tammy didn't hear her words but could tell that Harriet was attracted to Edgar. Smiling she said, "Come on, Harriet, it's time to feed the beast."

Harriet turned to the door and smiled at Tammy on her way out. Before closing the door Tammy gave Edgar a nod and mouthed the word, "Later."

Edgar watched the women as they continued down the sidewalk, when they entered The Cauldron, he turned back to his office.

There really wasn't any work he needed to do; at the same time, he had no reason to rush home. Instead, he stretched out on a small cot and set an alarm for ninety-minutes.

They'll be back tonight, and I need to know what Tammy's up to. Molly will want to know why she's back in town.

# CHAPTER 5

As we entered the restaurant I watched Tammy closely, something was off. I knew something was bothering her. I just didn't know what it was.

If I could read minds, I would have known she was thinking, "Please, Goddess don't let Mirabel be working tonight. I really want to surprise her at her cottage later tonight."

It was just past six thirty and I didn't see a sign giving the hours of The Cauldron. Once everyone was seated, I excused myself to go to the ladies' room. On my way I spotted a woman who looked like she was in charge.

"Excuse me."

"Yes, ma'am. How may I help you?"

"Are you the manager?"

"Yes, I am. My name is Sybil. Is there a problem?"

Smiling, I said, "No, Sybil." Nodding toward our table, "We've just arrived, and I don't know what time you close. I wouldn't want to overstay our welcome."

Sybil's smile was warm and friendly. "It's not a problem, ma'am. You and your group are welcome to stay as long as you please."

"Excellent! Thank you."

I continued to the restroom, where I was happy to find a clean and tidy facility.

Knowing that I didn't have to worry about closing time, I could relax and enjoy the group and the food. Some restaurants are fussy about closing time meaning that everyone is out by that time.

When I returned to the table, Harriet asked, "Is it safe to eat here?"

I laughed and said, "Yes."

The expressions of the rest of the women at the table were confused. Harriet explained. "Larissa always checks out the restroom of a restaurant before she decides to eat there. If it's not clean enough, she won't eat there."

I shrugged and looked around the table. "Think about it the next time you stop to eat somewhere. If they don't keep the restroom clean, what else don't they keep clean?"

The conversation moved on to what everyone was going to order. It was decided that we would each order something different and everyone would get a taste of each meal ordered.

When the meals were delivered Harriet said, "Please, just put everything in the middle of the table and bring five empty plates."

While the server, Donna, was no doubt confused her expression never showed it, nor did her response to the request.

"Yes, ma'am. Right away."

When my group arrived at the restaurant the only other people in the place was a young couple in a back corner. Once they departed, we had the place to ourselves.

Conversation during the meal centered on the food and the opportunity that each of us had to try different things.

As our server was clearing some of the dishes from the table, I asked, "Would it be possible to get a large decaf coffee to go?"

"Yes, ma'am." Her eyes swept the other ladies at the table. "Is there anything I can get for anyone else?"

Harriet asked, "What desserts are available?"

"Pumpkin pie, apple pie, carrot cake, and pumpkin cheesecake with a raspberry drizzle."

Harriet took a quick look around the table at everyone before answering, "Carrot cake and the cheesecake, with five forks. Oh, and I'd like some of that decaf too."

Tammy said, "Since we're having dessert, I'll take some decaf as well."

When the young lady brought the coffee, she delivered five filled mugs, left a thermal carafe, and five to go cups on the table. Before the coffee was cool enough to drink, the desserts were delivered.

It was well past nine when we departed The Cauldron. In addition to the tip left on the table, I slipped our young server a fifty-dollar bill.

Sara wanted to return to Edgar's shop. "We should all go get our cards read."

Beth chimed in with, "Yeah, sounds like fun."

I could tell that Harriet wasn't really interested in having her cards read; however, her earlier reaction to Edgar's baritone voice made it clear she wanted to go back to his shop.

"Really?" I sighed. "Okay, but I need to walk off some of dinner first."

Most of the shops had closed for the evening, so we window shopped our way down one side of the street and back up the other, until we found ourselves once again in front of Edgar's. I had been hoping that if I delayed our arrival long enough, he would be closed. No such luck.

As we approached Edgar's, I watched Tammy work her way to the front of the group. At his shop she held the door open for everyone else to enter. Which, just like our previous visit put her at the back of the group, closest to the door. I wondered why she wanted that specific location.

What is she up to? I know she's been to Cerridwen before.

"Welcome back ladies. What service may I offer you this evening?" His smile exposed white teeth beneath his pencil thin mustache. But the smile never reached his eyes, which made me instantly suspicious of him.

I moved away from the group and Edgar. While I pretended to look at his rock and crystal collection, I watched Tammy. She looked uncomfortable, almost afraid.

As it turns out I should have been keeping an eye on Harriet because the next thing I know she's volunteered me for a card reading.

"I think our hostess for the weekend should have a reading."

I wrapped my hand around the lovely blue stone with white veins that I'd been admiring and turned to face Harriet. If looks could kill, she would have dropped stone dead at that moment. But she didn't and I calmly placed the stone back where I'd found it instead of throwing it at her.

Harriet, my dear, I'll get you back for this. Oh well, it's all in fun and I won't be giving him any clues to work with. Let's see what he comes up with.

23

Edgar motioned for me to follow him through the curtains to a small room behind the glass counter. It's a good thing my claustrophobia isn't severe because the room was small and darker than the main portion of the shop.

"Please, be seated."

I thought about being an ass and sitting in the chair that was obviously meant for Edgar. Then I decided that would only delay the inevitable and I sat in the metal folding chair Edgar indicated. I closed my eyes for about ten seconds. When I opened them, the room didn't seem as dark as it had earlier.

Edgar was seated on the other side of the square cloth covered table. In the center of the cloth was an image of the Tree of Life. It was surrounded by the twelve Zodiac symbols, with a pentagram at the base of the tree. At the top of the tree, he placed a Tarot deck.

"Before we begin, I need to know what question you want the cards to answer. It shouldn't be a yes or no type of question. Something broader."

I inhaled deeply of the clove and cinnamon scented air and focused on the card deck. "Is there a lasting love in my future?" I brought my eyes up to meet Edgar's. "Broad enough for you?"

Holding my gaze, his face expressionless, he placed the deck in the center of the Tree of Life, and said, "Cut the deck into three stacks."

I kept my eyes on him as I cut the deck. He started collecting the cards with the third stack I'd created, and our hands brushed for the briefest moment.

I pulled my hand away as if I had been shocked. Edgar's eyes glazed over for a moment. Then he shuddered and drew in a long deep breath as if he'd been holding his breath for a long time.

He kept his eyes on the deck in his hand with an occasional furtive glance at me.

For my part, I continued to tell myself it had been nothing more than static electricity caused by the carpeting and the weather conditions.

I would learn later that Edgar was a psychic who didn't use his powers because he seldom liked what he saw. In my case, the contact was so brief that he only got a flash. Sadly, the flash was of death, fear, and pain.

"You've been hurt in the past and…" Edgar started with what I figured was the standard spiel. I could tell he was a bit off balance, though I didn't know why.

I laughed. "Do you know any adult who hasn't been?"

He placed another card on the table. "There is a woman you care a great deal for."

Another card. "You're not sure if she feels the same." Another card. "She has a dangerous job and…"

"Stop!" I took a split second to mentally review what each of the women in the other room knew about me and decided the only one who could have supplied Edgar with the information he was supposedly reading in the cards was Harriet. "Been talking to Harriet, haven't you?"

"Who?"

"The innocent act won't work with me. There's no other way you could know all that."

Edgar brought his hand to his heart. "You wound me."

Leaning forward I held his gaze. "Bullshit! I saw the look of recognition in your eyes when we were in here earlier. You know one of the women in my group. Somehow, she signaled you to keep quiet. To not let on that you know her."

Edgar studied me for several moments. "Yes. I know one of the women in your group. But when would she have had a chance to tell me anything about you?" He shrugged. "You all left here together, and I presume you ate at The Cauldron, again together."

I nodded.

Smiling he continued, "The Cauldron has no Wi-Fi. At least not for patrons. That crazy old bat likes to pretend that it's because the spirits don't want people on their phones. So, unless you believe in telepathy, there's no way she could have sent me information from the restaurant." He leaned back in his chair. "Do you believe in telepathy?"

"Every one of them knew at least 48 hours ahead of time where we were going this weekend."

Edgar sighed. "Alas, I see I'm not going to convince you that I have received no fore knowledge of you. Everything I've told you this evening is what the cards reveal."

"Sure, it was." I shrugged, dropped two twenty-dollar bills on the table, and extended my hand. "No hard feelings. It's all just for fun. Right?"

Edgar fidgeted in his chair and didn't reach to shake my hand.

I withdrew my hand. "Germaphobe? No problem. A lot of people don't like to shake hands. How about a fist bump?" He actually looked afraid to touch me.

He refused to meet my eyes and stood up abruptly, spun toward the curtain and pulled it back. It took a moment for my eyes to adjust to the new light level. By the time I could see again, Edgar was at the front door, holding it open.

"Good evening, ladies. I'm closing now." His smile looked forced. "Come back another time and I'll do a reading for each of you, at a discount. But right now, I must go."

As we exited the building, I saw Edgar whisper something to Tammy.

On the sidewalk outside Edgar's shop, we all looked at one another trying to figure out why we were given the bums rush.

Sara laughed. "Probably just a dramatic ploy that he hopes will have us coming back at a more convenient time." She glanced at her watch. "It is kind of late."

I looked at Tammy, deciding whether I would ask her about Edgar now or later, when we were alone. I opted for later and said, "Well, I've had enough hocus pocus for one evening. I'm headed to Ravenswood and bed. What about the rest of you?"

Harriet decided that she was going to go to the bar at the local hotel, the Crescent Moon, for a nightcap. Sara and Beth decided to go with her.

Tammy and I walked back to Ravenswood in silence. With the large oaks hanging over the road and no streetlights, the flashlights Amanda had given us were quite welcome.

Inside our room, I leaned against the door. Tammy was across the room staring out the window.

"How long have you known Edgar?"

Tammy spun around and faced me. She didn't have a very good poker face. "What makes you think I know Edgar?"

"What did Edgar say to you as he was chasing us out of his shop?" I asked walking into the room.

I could see the wheels turning in her head as she decided about what she was going to say. She bristled and obviously decided on being indignant and angry.

She crossed her arms over her chest as she stepped toward me.

"First you accuse me of knowing this Edgar person and now you think he's passing me secret messages. You sound like a jealous lover. Remember, we're not a couple. We're friends who occasionally have sex."

I glanced at the bed. There will be no sex tonight. At least not between us.

Her bag was still on the bench at the foot of the bed. She hadn't taken time to unpack before we went to dinner. I walked to the dresser and grabbed the key to the room down the hall. Tossing it to Tammy I said, "That's for the third room down the hall. You can have anyone that you want to join you. I'm going down to the garden for a walk. When I get back, be next door, be gone" I shrugged "just don't be here."

Tammy caught the key and looked from it to me to her bag. She grabbed her bag and without a word walked around me and out the door.

I expected her to slam the door, so I was surprised when she left it open. I moved to the doorway intending to close it but stopped when I saw her standing at the top of the stairs looking down. Then she looked down the hallway at the door I'd just given her the key to and glanced back down the stairs before turning to unlock her room.

As she moved down the hall I listened, when I heard her enter the room, I closed the door to my room.

I flopped on the bed and stared at the ceiling thinking, "I hope the rest of the group is having a good time."

# CHAPTER 6

Tammy waited a few minutes and then slipped downstairs. She knew Amanda would be in the kitchen working on pastries or bread for the next morning's breakfast. She avoided the third step from the bottom, she knew squeaked.

She stepped into the kitchen, where, as she had anticipated, Amanda was working a sizeable amount of dough.

"Thanks for not giving me up." Amanda looked at her as if she didn't understand. "You know, for not letting the others know that we know each other."

Amanda slammed the dough she was working with on the countertop. "That's your business. I'm just curious, why don't you want the others to know that you used to live in Cerridwen?"

Tammy looked around the kitchen. "I'm not sure. Is Mirabel okay?"

"As far as I know. Why?"

"Just had a weird feeling all afternoon." She held Amanda's gaze.

Amanda thought back to the horrible wave of disorientation that washed over her when she was greeting Larissa and

Harriet. The last time I had that feeling…No! I can't think about that.

"I know Mirabel told you that she's thinking about coming to stay with me in Central City. What do you think about the idea?"

"It doesn't matter what I think. It's her life and her decision, to stay or go." Tammy waited; she knew Amanda wasn't finished. "But since you asked for my opinion, I think she'll be unhappy in the city. More unhappy in the city than you were here."

Tammy sighed. "Sadly, I think you're right. I'm going to go see her later tonight." She paused, then asked worriedly, "You didn't tell her I was here, did you?"

Laughing Amanda said, "I think you know me better than that."

Looking relieved Tammy said, "Right. I guess I do." Changing the subject she asked, "How's Cassandra?"

Amanda smiled, she adored her daughter and was always willing to talk about her. "She spends a lot of time with Mirabel learning about plants. Cassandra says Mirabel tells her she's a natural and a quick study." Continuing to knead the dough Amanda smiled and added, "I can't believe she's almost seventeen." Shaking her head, she said, "I'm certainly going to miss her when she goes off to college."

"Where's she thinking of going?"

"She's applied to several. All of them are close enough that she can live here and commute. The last time we talked she said she was going to accept whichever one would allow her to do most, if not all, of her classes online."

"Really?"

"Yes, most kids can't wait to go away to college. My daughter is trying to find a college that will let her stay home." Looking up from her dough she looked at Tammy. "And I'm not sure if it's because she wants to stay with me or if she doesn't want to be away from Mirabel."

"Hmm. Well, if Mirabel comes to the city and Cass decides to go off to college, you'll have your answer."

Amanda had just sprinkled flour on her lump of dough, and she flicked her flour covered hand toward Tammy, who jumped back. The flour cloud fell short of its target.

Both women laughed and Amanda said, "You haven't changed a bit."

Hearing someone coming down the stairs Tammy said, "I'll let you know how my visit with Mirabel goes."

Cassandra stepped into the kitchen. "Hello Tammy."

"Hi, kiddo. Wow! You've certainly grown since the last time I saw you." She looked at Amanda. "What are you feeding this girl? She has to have grown six inches."

Cassandra's expression never changed as she, kissed her mother on the cheek, nodded toward Tammy and said, "I've finished putting the linens away and I'm going to bed."

"Goodnight sweetie."

"Goodnight, Cassandra."

Cassandra nodded toward Tammy in a non-verbal goodnight.

An awkward tension that entered the room with Cassandra stayed after her departure.

Tammy cleared her throat, "I think I'll go take a quick nap before I head to the cottage."

# CHAPTER 7

Taking a walk in the garden had seemed like a good idea
when I said it, but then the bed called my name. I looked at
the time and realized it was a bit late for joining the others in
town. By the time I'd get there they would probably be ready
to head back to the manor.

I lay there staring at the ceiling, thinking I should probably
brush my teeth and change for bed.

"What!?" I sat up and looked around the room. Checking the
time, I realized I must have dozed off. It was nearly an hour
since I laid down.

I stretched and looked out the window. The moon hadn't
risen yet.

If memory serves me, the moon won't rise until sometime
after three a.m.

Opening the door and stepping out on the balcony, the crisp
cool October air was refreshing. I took a deep breath and
exhaled slowly. Looking the length of the balcony, I noticed
that all the rooms had access to it and like at my end, there
were stairs at the opposite end leading to the garden.

Below in the garden the only light was from the solar
powered lights that dotted the footpaths that wove their way
around the trees, flower beds, and fountains.

Then suddenly there was a burst of light at the other end of the garden.

Hmm. Security light must have been tripped. Probably some witch's cat out for a stroll.

"Bollocks!"

Tammy! She must be the one who tripped the light. Where is she going at this hour?

I scanned the garden.

There was no way she's moved into the garden without me being able to see her.

As quickly as it had come on the light went out. I closed my eyes, covered them with a hand, and counted to seven. This sped up their adjustment to the reduced light.

When I opened my eyes and searched the garden, I saw a shadowy form moving toward the back.

Without pausing to close my door I descended the stairs at my end of the balcony. As I reached the last step a light came on. Anticipating this, I moved to my right, ducking behind a tall bush. Through the foliage I watched Tammy stop and look in my direction before continuing toward the gate.

Once Tammy turned away, I moved deeper into the garden being careful to stay behind bushes tall enough to conceal me. As soon as the light went out, I stopped, and again squeezed my eyes shut, covered them with my hands, and counted to seven before uncovering and opening them.

While my eyes were closed, I heard a squeak. She's gone out the gate. Where the devil is she going?

At the gate I leaned over and looked to my right. Nothing. Then I looked to the left. There I saw a shadow being led down the dirt road by a small circle of light.

Has to be Tammy, using her flashlight.

I reached down and checked the pocket of my cargo pants and breathed a sigh of relief when my hand touched the flashlight from Amanda.

Knowing that the gate squeaked when opened, I waited until I thought Tammy was far enough away that she wouldn't hear it. Then I pulled the latch and quickly opened and closed the gate.

As soon as the gate was closed, I moved away from it to the middle of the road and squatted down. She never paused to look back and I started after her.

Staying in the shadows I moved as quickly as I could in the dark. Once I got too close to a Bougainville and a thorn scratched my arm.

"Ow!" As soon as the word left my mouth I crouched down. Even though I knew I was probably visible, well, as visible as anything else on a dark dirt road with no moon and no ambient light from streetlights or buildings, I also knew that human nature would be to look for someone standing, not someone crouched down.

Tammy stopped and turned to look behind her. She aimed her flashlight in my direction.

She's probably wondering if she really heard someone or if her imagination is running wild.

I was far enough away that her flashlight was swallowed by the night before it reached me. She turned and continued down the winding dirt road.

I straightened up. Tammy had gone around a curve in the road, and I lost sight of her. Figuring that if I couldn't see her, she couldn't see me, I turned on my own flashlight. Shining it on my upper left arm, I saw a thin line of blood.

Well, at least it won't show on this black shirt.

Fearing I might be giving Tammy too much of a lead, I hurried forward.

Even though she was well ahead of me, at least I knew someone was out here with me. Being alone in the dark, surrounded by woods, the sounds of the night seemed magnified. The nighttime critters rustling about in the leaves, the wind moving the tree branches and the hanging moss. A chill ran up my spine and I moved quickly to catch up to her.

Soon there was another hairpin turn in the dirt road and I could see the back of the shops on this side of Ravens Road. Looking between the buildings I could see streetlights. Until that moment I hadn't realized how really tense I'd been, navigating the darkness.

If I continued forward, I would be in downtown Cerridwen. If I went either left or right, the road ran the length of the buildings.

There was no sign of Tammy. If she'd gone either left or right, I'd probably still be able to see her. She must have gone into town.

But why? All the shops are closed.

Then it hit me. That must be what Edgar whispered to her. That she should come back at a certain time.

Hugging the wall of the nearest building I looked out on the main street of Cerridwen. Ravens Road was empty.

Damn it, I've lost her.

Then in the distance I heard a computerized voice, "Step back. You are too close to the vehicle. Step back. You are too close to the vehicle. If you do not back away from the vehicle an alarm will sound in five, four…" The countdown stopped.

A car alarm. Hopefully, it was Tammy that triggered it and not some vampire or such. Wow! Really, vampires. My imagination is definitely running wild.

I raced across the street, hurrying to the back of the buildings on the other side. I arrived at the edge of a well-lit parking lot just in time to see Tammy push through the hedge of low bushes on the far side and disappear into the woods.

Running across the parking lot I was careful to cross the hedge away from the car that Tammy had been nearest. I certainly don't want the alarm going off, like it had for her.

I followed the footpath on the far side of the hedge to where she had disappeared. There was a path leading into the woods. In the distance I could see a light, then it disappeared.

Must have been her flashlight. She either turned it off or went around a bend. Not one of these damn paths has been straight.

Keeping my flashlight pointed at the ground, I headed down the path. It seemed to be well-traveled, as there weren't a lot of roots or debris to trip over, making my progress faster.

Just before rounding each bend, I turned my flashlight off, moved cautiously, around the turn, and surveyed the area ahead of me. Coming around the most recent turn in the path, I could make out the shadow of a house against the night sky. Then the lights in the house came on.

I moved down the path another twenty feet, paused at the edge of the woods and crouched down behind a bush.

In front of me was a well-tended yard and garden. The night air carried the aroma of Rosemary to me, and I inhaled deeply. It's one of my favorite smells.

Tammy must have brushed against it when she crossed the yard.

Before I could decide what to do next, Tammy burst out of the house running blindly, she trampled a plot of Marigolds and was headed straight for me. I stood up, blocking her entrance to the path away from the house.

At first it was as if she didn't recognize me. "Who...What...It's you. What the bloody hell are you doing here?"

I raised an eyebrow. "I might ask you the same thing." I paused and studied Tammy's face. It was pale and she looked terrified.

"What's wrong? I can't help you if I don't know what the problem is."

Tammy took a ragged breath, let it out slowly, and took another before bringing her eyes up to meet mine. "The problem is that...the problem is that Mirabel's..."

"Mirabel? Who is Mirabel?" I glanced at the house and then brought my attention back to Tammy. "Is this Mirabel's house?"

Tammy nodded. "Yes." The word was barely audible.

"So, what's the problem with Mirabel?"

Tammy looked over her shoulder at the house, as she said, "She's gone."

"Were you supposed to meet her, and she stood you up?"

Looking into my eyes, Tammy said, "No, I mean she's – gone."

"Gone?" I inhaled sharply and quietly asked, "You mean she's…dead?"

Tammy nodded.

"Are you sure she's not just unconscious?"

"Yes." Tammy was beginning to get herself under control. "I touched her neck, looking for a pulse. There was none and she was cold."

I quickly weighed a variety of scenarios. Natural causes? Maybe. I know Tammy didn't kill her. She wasn't far enough ahead of me to have had time for that. Unless she killed her earlier and knew I was following her, and we would have this scene. No, Tammy's not that complex.

"Wait here." I started for the house.

"Where are you going?"

Looking at Tammy I said, "I'm going to see for myself. Wait here."

When Tammy ran out of the house, she hadn't turned off the lights or closed the door behind her. This allowed me to use my shoulder to push the door open all the way and step into the kitchen of the house.

Moving into the kitchen I was careful where I stepped. I didn't want Det. Murdoch to be able to say I compromised her crime scene. I kept my hands in my pockets, to avoid accidentally touching anything. I walked to the far side of the kitchen island and on the floor next to it lay a woman curled up in the fetal position.

There was no blood and no obvious signs of how the woman died. I bent down and using my shirt tail I lifted a finger on the corpse.

Hmmm. Rigor mortis hasn't set in so less than twelve hours. It's twelve-fifteen now. So she died sometime in the afternoon.

The kitchen door slammed shut and I jumped up. For an instant panic flooded my mind. The fight or flight instinct reared its ugly head. There was no one to fight and a variety of directions to run. I took a long slow breath to calm myself.

The wind must have blown it shut.

While I was still deciding whether to look around some more or leave, the door opened.

Thank the Goddess. It was only Tammy.

Tammy stood in the doorway, showing no interest in entering the cottage. Without hesitating I stepped back around the kitchen island and ushered her back outside. Again, using the tail of my shirt I pulled the door closed.

Moving toward the trail back the way we'd come, I pulled out my phone. "Crap. I don't have any bars here. As soon as we get back to the manor, I need to call Murdoch."

"Who's Murdoch?"

"She's a detective for the Hamilton County Sheriff's Department."

Tammy stopped in her tracks. "What the bloody hell for? Are you bonkers? Why are you going to call the coppers?"

I put my phone away and studied Tammy. "Did you kill her?"

"What!?! No, I didn't kill her."

"Then why do you object to the police being notified?"

"It's just...well, I don't know. It just seems like..."

"Seems like what?"

Tammy sighed. "It just seems like asking for trouble."

I laughed. "Asking for trouble is not reporting and then they find out you knew about the dead body in the cottage in the woods. Come on, let's get somewhere I can use my phone."

# CHAPTER 8

As we headed back to the manor, I kept checking my phone for reception. In the parking lot behind the shops on Ravens Road I had enough bars to place a call.

Murdoch's sleepy voice said, "Hello Ms. Carpenter, what can I do for you?"

I cleared my throat, straightened my shoulders, and said, "Believe it or not, I need to report finding a body." Silence. "Detective?"

"Seriously?" Murdoch's voice was incredulous. "Ms. Carpenter, you report more dead bodies to me than the 911 dispatcher. Is this a hobby of yours?" I heard her sigh. "Where is it?"

"Cerridwen. Meet me at Ravenswood Manor." I ended the call without waiting for a reply.

"Come on, Tammy. Let's get back to the manor."

"Why did you follow me?"

"I was curious about where you might be going in the middle of the night. Nothing more." I paused. "Who was Mirabel?"

Tammy hesitated before answering. "A friend. I hadn't seen her in a while."

"So, you thought dropping in unannounced at midnight was a good idea."

"Mirabel is…was a night owl and I wanted to surprise her."

"Unfortunately, I think you're the one that got the surprise."

Neither of us spoke for the rest of the walk back to the manor. I led Tammy up the stairs through the still open door to my room. She plopped into the first chair she came to. The color still hadn't returned to her face. I poured her a double of Blanton's bourbon.

"Drink that and lie down for a bit. Sleep if you can."

Tammy downed the drink in one large gulp, got up and walked to the bed, and laid down on top of the covers. I took her shoes off, put them on the floor next to the bed, and threw a blanket over her.

"I'm going to go let Amanda know what's going on."

As I headed for the ground floor, I tried to come up with the best way to tell Amanda about the dead woman in the cottage in the woods.

Shit! Sounds like the title of a B horror movie. The dead woman in the cottage in the woods.

As I reached the last step, Amanda seemed to appear out of nowhere.

She wore an expression of deep concern. "What's happened?"

I looked at the distraught woman, wondering how she could have known that something had happened. This place really is a bit on the spooky side.

"Do you know the woman in the cottage on the far side of town?"

"Yes. Mirabel. Is she ill?"

"No. I'm afraid, she's dead. I've already called Detective Murdoch. She's on her way."

"Mirabel. Dead." She shook her head as she moved into the kitchen, muttering to herself.

I followed her and asked, "Did you know her well?"

"Yes. She is…was a member of our coven." Amanda watched me, as if she were looking for a reaction to her statement. Over the years I have developed an excellent poker face and it helped that Tammy told me a while back that she was a witch.

"How did she die?"

"I don't know. There were no obvious signs of injury." I paused. "I imagine there'll be an autopsy."

Amanda put a kettle on the stove and began setting out things for tea.

"I'm going to wait out front for the detective." I started out, paused, and asked, "Did the rest of my group get back from town?"

"Yes, they came in a little past twelve." She looked up at the ceiling. "I imagine they're all asleep by now."

While I waited for Murdoch, I thought about the fact that Amanda hadn't asked me anything about how I found the body. She didn't question that a person new to Cerridwen had been at Mirabel's cottage in the middle of the night. Curious.

# CHAPTER 9

Murdoch sat on the edge of her bed looking at her cell phone. Cerridwen. Interesting town, though not a place I expected to find Larissa Carpenter. What the hell is she doing there?

An hour later Murdoch pulled up in front of Ravenswood Manor.

"Good morning, detective." Having made a concerted effort to avoid running into the detective, it had been a several weeks since Larissa had seen Murdoch.

Her mouth went dry, and her stomach was filled with butterflies at the sight of the woman.

Damn it! I'd hoped that not seeing her would cure me of this nonsense.

"Good morning, Ms. Carpenter." She studied Larissa, thinking how much she would like to kiss her. She cleared her throat, mentally chastising herself for such an unprofessional thought.

She started to get out of the car. "Where's the body? Inside?"

"No, it's in a cottage in the woods on the other side of town." Larissa headed for the passenger side of Murdoch's car.

"We'll only be able to take your car part of the way." She climbed into the front seat. "After that we'll have to walk."

"Great." Murdoch got back behind the wheel and started the car. "Just how did you stumble upon this body?"

"Head out of here as if you were going into town. Before you reach the first set of shops, you'll see a road to the left with a sign that says parking. Follow that to the parking lot. From there we'll have to walk."

Murdoch repeated the directions to ensure she had them right. "Now that I know where I'm going, tell me how you found this body."

Larissa explained about the girls' weekend. "Well, Harriet, Sara, Beth, Tammy, and I decided it would be fun to spend the weekend here. You know so close to All Hallows Eve and all."

Murdoch noticed that she hadn't called it Halloween. "Yeah, and…"

Larissa sighed. "I was out on the balcony enjoying the view of the gardens, when I noticed Tammy slipping across the garden and out the gate." She shrugged. "I was curious, so I followed her. She wasn't in this cottage more than a minute when she came tearing out like she'd seen a ghost."

"And of course, you had to go and look for yourself, didn't you?"

"For your information Detective Murdoch, I kept my hands in my pockets. I didn't disturb your crime scene and as soon as I got where my cell phone had reception, I called you."

Murdoch grunted. "Does Tammy have a last name and where is she now?"

46

"Yes, she does. Last I saw her she was in bed, after downing a double-shot of my Blanton's bourbon."

Murdoch drew in a long, calming breath before saying, "Let me rephrase that. What is Tammy's last name?"

Larissa smiled. She loved yanking Murdoch's chain. "Lopez. Tammy Lopez."

"What makes you think this woman's death wasn't natural?" Murdoch pulled into the parking lot.

"I suggest you stay at this end of the lot." She pointed to the sports car at the other end of the lot. "Tammy got too close to that car down there and it actually told her she was too close and if she didn't back off it would sound an alarm."

Murdoch parked two spots away from the indicated car, commenting, "Yeah, I don't think I want to wake everyone in town. At least, not yet." She turned in the seat to face Larissa. "Are you going to answer my question?"

Larissa stared out the windshield for a couple of seconds before saying, "What makes me think the death wasn't natural?"

"Yeah."

Facing Murdoch she said, "Honestly, I don't know. She just looked like she was in a lot of pain when she died."

"Natural or not, death can be quite painful" Murdoch said as she got out of the car.

Standing next to the car, Murdoch answered her phone. "Murdoch. Yeah, where are you? Okay, turn left onto Ravens Road. Before you reach the actual town, you'll see a road to the left that leads to a parking lot." She paused. "I'll have someone meet you there to guide you to the scene. Oh yeah and stay away from the sports car" she smiled "unless you want to wake up the town. See you soon."

Murdoch put away her phone and turned to Larissa. "Lead on."

Flashlights in hand the two women entered the woods. The path was just wide enough for them to walk side-by-side. As they were approaching the last bend in the trail, Murdoch said, "This is a rather out of the way place. Obviously, Tammy knew this woman."

"I think they used to be lovers."

Murdoch chuckled and shook her head.

"What?" Larissa asked.

They were approaching the cottage and Murdoch stopped and looked at Larissa. "How do you keep getting into these situations?"

With a faint smile Larissa looked at Murdoch and tilted her head. "Right place, right time or wrong place, wrong time." She shrugged. "I haven't decided which it is, yet. What do you think?"

Instead of answering her, Murdoch sighed and started forward.

As they crossed the yard, Murdoch noted the well-kept garden, including the plot of Marigolds Tammy had trampled in her haste to get away from the cottage. Standing at the door to the kitchen, she stopped and shone her flashlight around the outside of the small house. A path of steppingstones to the left led around to the other side of the cottage.

Indicating the path she asked, "Did you go back there?"

"No. I hadn't noticed it before now."

Larissa followed Murdoch as she moved down this new path, shining her flashlight on the ground, as she looked for evidence of anyone else having been there recently.

The path was made of closely placed steppingstones, so there wasn't any soil for footprints. Occasionally, Murdoch paused and examined the ground between the path and the cottage. Larissa mirrored her actions on the opposite side of the path.

On the side Larissa was examining was a swath of yard about ten feet wide and then the woods took over. Murdoch's side of the path was grass too, though much narrower.

As they rounded the corner of the cottage, the path met a driveway. Murdoch played her flashlight down the driveway. The dirt road at the end was barely visible. She grunted and brought her flashlight back to guide her feet.

On the other side of the driveway the path continued around the house to another door. Looking through the window near the door they could see the living room to the right and at the opposite end of the cottage on the other side was the kitchen.

Murdoch tried the front door. Locked. "You say the kitchen door's unlocked?"

"Yeah."

"All right." Without another word Murdoch headed back around the building.

Back at the door to the kitchen, Murdoch pulled a pair of booties from a pocket, before putting them on over her shoes, she turned to Larissa. "Can I get you to do something for me?"

"Sure."

"Go back to the parking lot and guide the ME and the forensics team here. They're probably there already and wondering where I'm at." She checked her phone. "I'm surprised I haven't gotten a call." She put her phone away.

"Yeah, sure."

"Thanks." Murdoch put the booties on and a pair of blue gloves. Then she opened the door and started using her phone as a video recorder.

Larissa tuned and headed back to the parking lot.

# CHAPTER 10

Standing just inside the kitchen doorway Murdoch activated the video camera on her phone, slowly panning from left to right, and talking as she went.

"Round table with four chairs. The kitchen is open to the rest of the house. Across the hall is a door, presumably leading to the garage. The north wall of the kitchen has cabinets from floor to just below the ceiling."

She stepped forward and opened all the cabinet doors, revealing canned and dry goods, spices, jars of dried herbs, and a variety of small kitchen appliances.

"Basically, what one would expect to find in a kitchen pantry." She closed the doors, stepped back, and turned to her right. "Large kitchen island. No appliances on it. Looks clean. Opposite the island is a refrigerator, counter space, stove, and oven. Next to that is a large country sink and then more counter space."

She walked around the island and there on the floor was Mirabel's body. Before moving in for a close up of the body, Murdoch videoed the top of the counters, the empty sink, and the empty dish rack with drainboard.

"Either Mirabel didn't prepare meals here or she was fanatical about cleaning up afterward."

Making sure she got the entire floor area around the body; Murdoch slowly moved the camera around. Then she circled the island and videoed the body from the other direction. After that she turned off the video and took close up still shots of the body.

Squatting next to the body, Murdoch examined it as closely as she could without touching it. She sniffed the air.

Faint smell of mint.

Then she examined the floor in the immediate vicinity, her flashlight passed over something that sparkled. Taking a closer look Murdoch saw it was a small glass shard. It looked like there was something dried on it.

She videoed and photographed it in place, then put it in an evidence bag. Standing up she pulled a marker from a pocket and wrote the date, time, and location where the item was found on the bag, along with her initials. Then she placed the bag in a pocket.

Next, she opened the cabinet under the sink. The smell of mint was overpowering.

She pulled a small trash receptable out and videoed its contents.

Looks like a broken glass and it has something dried on it too. The piece I already found must have been missed when she cleaned up. Whatever was in that broken glass must be where the mint smell is coming from.

Murdoch straightened up and looked around. She felt like she was being watched but it was clear that she was alone, except for the corpse.

She put the trash can back where she'd found it, turned off her video recording, and moved toward the hallway.

Standing where the kitchen and the hallway met to her left was a double bi-fold door. Behind it was a washer and dryer. Above the appliances was a wire shelf. A couple of blouses were hanging from the shelf. She closed the door and opened the door on the opposite wall.

As she had suspected it opened to a garage. There was no car. There was a bicycle. The tires were fat, well-suited for traversing the path from the parking lot. A large basket on the front and saddlebags over the rear fender. Like the house, the garage was exceptionally clean. Murdoch closed the door and walked down the hall.

On her left was a living room. Couch a couple of chairs. A coffee table and an end table. The wall the room shared with the garage was lined with bookshelves.

Interesting there's not a television anywhere.

To her right was an open door to the bedroom. The bed was made. The room was tidy. She opened the closet and found that it was organized. Short sleeve shirts were hung with short sleeve shirts. Long sleeve shirts were hung with long sleeve shirts. Blue jeans were draped over hangers and grouped together. When she opened dresser drawers, she found they too were organized to the extreme.

When she stepped into the bathroom, she wasn't at all surprised to find that it too was clean and without any clutter on the counter.

"Detective Murdoch?"

Excellent the ME is here. "Yes, Dr. Cameron." Murdoch entered the kitchen to see Dr. Cameron standing next to the body with a sour look on her face.

"Have you touched the body?" Her tone was accusatory.

Murdoch stiffened. "This isn't my first rodeo, Dr. Cameron. No, I didn't touch the body."

Dr. Cameron didn't say anything. She squatted down next to the corpse and began her examination.

"Any idea how long she's been dead?"

Cameron moved a finger on the corpse. "Close to twelve hours. Rigor's just beginning."

"Hmmm." Murdoch checked the time and scribbled in her notebook. "So sometime around four yesterday afternoon."

Cameron rolled Mirabel onto her back and straightened her out

"When will the postmortem be ready?"

Murdoch waited several seconds for a reply before saying, "Sorry if I was a little brusque earlier." Smiling, she continued, "Sam and I had a good working relationship and I hope that you and I will have a similar relationship."

Dr. Cameron stood up, her face expressionless and staring at Murdoch said, "I am not Sam. I have no knowledge of your experience with corpses at crime scenes. And you'll have the postmortem when I've finished the autopsy." Without another word she returned to her examination of the body.

The assistant with Cameron tried to make himself as invisible as possible. He didn't want to witness this, and he also didn't want to be Cameron's next target. He'd already experienced the woman's cold anger.

Murdoch's face turned red with fury, and she stormed out of the cottage. Larissa was waiting for her outside. It was obvious she had heard every word of the exchange between Murdoch and Dr. Cameron.

54

The detective didn't say a word as she headed down the trail to the parking lot. Larissa was challenged to keep up with her long strides. Fortunately, she was in good shape and though her legs weren't as long as Murdoch's she stayed with her without getting out of breath.

As Murdoch started the engine, Larissa asked, "Did you tell them to check a map for a way to get a vehicle back there?"

An evil smile turned up the corners of Murdoch's mouth. "No. If they can't figure it out" she glanced at Larissa "I guess they'll have to carry the body to the parking lot."

Before she put the car in gear, she texted Cameron's assistant. Make sure to bag contents of trash can under sink.

# CHAPTER 11

As Murdoch and Larissa entered Ravenswood Manor, Larissa said, "I'll bring Tammy down to the living room." She pointed to the room to the left.

Murdoch was perusing book titles and running a finger down the spines of the books, almost in the manner one caresses a lover's face, when Amanda Colton entered the room with a hot mug of coffee. "I thought you might need this, Det. Murdoch."

The detective turned around and was presented with the mug of coffee. "I'm Amanda Colton. Welcome to Ravenswood Manor, though I wish it were under different circumstances."

"Yes, Ms. Colton. I remember you from a previous visit to Cerridwen. I'm sorry to say that it seems the only time I manage to make it to Cerridwen, is for something work related." Smiling, Murdoch accepted the mug and inhaled the aroma of fresh brewed coffee. "Did you know the deceased?"

"Yes, I did." She paused and then said, "Ms. Carpenter and Ms. Lopez are here."

Murdoch didn't see anyone at first and then the two women in question entered the room. "I'll leave you to your work detective."

Raising the mug in salute, Murdoch said, "Thanks for the coffee."

Tammy walked to one of the wingback chairs and plopped down. Larissa started to leave but Tammy said, "I'd rather you stayed."

Larissa looked at Murdoch. Murdoch looked at Tammy and said, "You're sure you wouldn't rather do this privately."

"I'm sure."

Murdoch nodded, indicated that Larissa should take the chair next to Tammy's and then sat down opposite her. She placed her phone on the table between them and said, "Unless you object Ms. Lopez, I'll be recording our interview."

"No objection."

"Very well. This interview is with Ms. Tammy Lopez regarding the death of Mirabel…Tammy what's Mirabel's last name?"

"Fleur. F, L, E, U, R."

"Thank you. This interview is regarding the death of Mirabel Fleur. The date is October 22, 2022. The time is 3:31 a.m. Also present is Ms. Larissa Carpenter. She's here at Ms. Lopez's request. Ms. Lopez, why were you going to see Ms. Fleur?"

Tammy's voice was barely audible as she began, "Mirabel and I were friends…"

"Ms. Lopez, I'm going to need you to speak up a bit."

Tammy cleared her throat and sat up straighter. "Mirabel and I were friends. I hadn't seen her in a while and since I was in Cerridwen I figured I'd drop by for a visit."

"In the middle of the night?"

"Mirabel didn't keep the same hours as most people. I was surprised that the cottage was dark when I got there." She leaned forward and rested her elbows on her thighs, with her hands clasped in front of her. "I tried the kitchen door and as I expected it was unlocked." She licked her lips and took a deep breath. "I stepped in, turned on the lights, and…"

"And that's when you saw Ms. Fleur on the floor?"

Tammy leaned back in the chair again. "Well, yeah when I stepped around the island." She jumped up from the chair and began pacing. "I've never seen a dead body before."

"Please, be seated, Ms. Lopez."

"Yeah, sure." Tammy sat back down.

"What did you do next?"

"I opened the refrigerator, got myself a beer, and… I got the bloody hell out of there. What the bloody hell do you think I did?"

"Did you touch anything in the kitchen besides the light switch?"

"I…I don't think so." She paused. "I…I might have grabbed the counter. I felt a bit unsteady." She was sitting on the edge of the chair, holding her head in her hands.

"We'll need to fingerprint you." Tammy jerked her head up and looked at Murdoch. "It's so we can eliminate your prints from whatever others we find." This seemed to satisfy Tammy and she relaxed. "What happened next, once you were outside?"

Tammy took another deep breath and exhaled sharply. "I ran into Larissa at the trailhead."

"And?" Getting this woman to talk is like pulling teeth without anesthesia.

"She asked me what was wrong. I told her and she went inside to look for herself."

Murdoch looked at Larissa as she asked, "How long was she in the cottage?"

"Bloody hell, what do you think I had a stopwatch going? How should I know?" She paused and took a couple of deep breaths, while Murdoch waited. "She wasn't long. The wind slammed the kitchen door." Tammy smiled and looked at Larissa. "Bet that made you jump."

Larissa said nothing and schooled her expression to give nothing away.

"Anyway, I went back and opened the door to see if she was all right. Then we headed here. Once we reached the parking lot, her phone had enough bars that she could call you."

Murdoch glanced down at the notes she had been taking during the interview. She brought her eyes up and held Tammy's gaze. "Let me see if I've got this right. You went out in the middle of the night to visit Ms. Fleur, found her dead on her kitchen floor, discovered you'd been followed there by Ms. Carpenter, who went inside to see for herself. Then the two of you came back here." She paused. "Is that accurate?"

"Yeah. Look I'm really knackered, mind if I go back to Bedfordshire?" Tammy stood up.

Murdoch's confused expression amused Larissa. "No, I'm afraid you can't leave the area, you're…"

Smiling Larissa said, "Murdoch, knackered is tired and Bedfordshire is, well, bed. She's tired and wants to go back to bed."

"Oh, of course." Murdoch rose and handed Tammy a card. "If you think of anything or of anyone who might have wanted to harm Ms. Fleur, please let me know."

Tammy was a bit wobbly on her feet and Larissa got up to help her upstairs.

"Before you go, Tammy. What time did you arrive here yesterday?"

"I think it was around five thirty."

Murdoch looked at Larissa for confirmation. "Yes, she was the last of the group to arrive. Five thirty sounds about right."

"Ms. Carpenter, once you have her tucked in, please, come back. I have some questions for you."

# CHAPTER 12

I started to take Tammy to my room, then I changed my mind and took her to her own room. It's just less complicated this way.

As I was removing Tammy's shoes, I asked, "Why didn't you tell the detective that you and Mirabel were once lovers?"

Still fully clothed, Tammy flopped back on the bed. "She didn't ask. Please, just let me be."

I sighed and studied Tammy's face for a moment, the pain of loss was easy to see. I headed back to Murdoch and her questions.

Partway down the stairs, I paused and took a deep breath before continuing down, making a point of avoiding the third step from the bottom. It was a squeaker.

Standing in the doorway to the study, I watched Murdoch.

What is it about this woman? Yes, she's good looking but I've never been one to concentrate on a person's looks. There's something else about her that just makes me tingle. That is when she's not annoying the piss out of me.

My thoughts were interrupted when Murdoch noticed me and said, "You really don't need permission to enter the room, Ms. Carpenter."

A flash of anger came and went so quickly that I didn't have time to act on it, which was probably a good thing. Sighing I took the chair I'd been in earlier, even though I don't like to sit with my back to a door.

Murdoch activated the recording app on her phone and again went through the procedure of asking my permission to record the interview.

"Why did you follow Ms. Lopez?"

"I told you earlier. Curiosity."

"Hmmm. Why did you go into the cottage?"

"Curiosity."

Watching Murdoch's face, I could tell she was tempted to remind me about curiosity killing the cat, but she refrained. Probably because this was an official recorded interview.

"How long have you known Ms. Lopez?"

"A while. Few months I suppose."

"Where were all the other ladies during the evening?"

"I'm not sure. They may have still been in town. After we left Edgar's, Harriet, Sara, and Beth went to the hotel bar for a nightcap."

"Who is Edgar?"

Damn! I didn't mean to tell her about that.

"Edgar is a Tarot card reader. He has a shop in town. He knows one of the women in the group. I don't know which one. I suspect it's Harriet."

"Why do you think it's Harriet?"

"Just some things he said."

"What things?"

I rolled my eyes and moved forward on the chair. "First of all, Harriet insisted that he read my cards. Then during the

62

reading, he said some things that the only way he could know them was if Harriet had told him. None of the other ladies know me that well."

Murdoch smiled. "Or he could be the real deal."

"Seriously! You believe in all that hocus pocus stuff." I scooted back in the chair.

"Not really." She looked at her notes. "About what time did you part ways with the others?"

"I'm not sure. I imagine the credit card receipt from The Cauldron will help with the timeline but I'm guessing we left the restaurant around nine-fifteen, maybe nine thirty. We took the long way round town to Edgar's shop, so about ten, maybe fifteen minutes to get there." I paused as I calculated how much time the group was in Edgar's shop. "I'd say we got the bum's rush from Edgar somewhere between nine-forty-five and ten."

Murdoch looked up from her notebook, where she'd been scribbling.

"Why do you think Edgar suddenly wanted you all to leave?"

"I'm not sure."

I thought about telling Murdoch about the static electric shock and then decided that there really wasn't anything to tell.

"I have a question. Why are you taking notes when you're recording the interview?"

Murdoch looked at me and I could almost see the mental gears turning while she decided whether or not to answer my question. She pulled her lower lip into her mouth for a moment and then said, "Because I don't trust technology."

Without missing a beat, she asked, "What time did you and Tammy arrive back here at the manor?"

"Tammy and I were back here by 10:30 p.m. Shortly after that I gave Tammy the key to her room, and I lay down on the bed. I must have fallen asleep for a bit. Because I know it was after eleven when I stepped out on the balcony."

Tammy has her own room. I was sure she and Larissa were sleeping together.

"What makes you think that Ms. Lopez and Ms. Fleur were at one time lovers?"

"I wasn't really sure until just a bit ago. When I was, as you put it, tucking Tammy into bed I asked her why she hadn't told you that she and Mirabel used to be lovers. She said it was because you didn't ask."

"Hmmm. What's Sara's last name?"

"Fisher and Elizabeth's last name is Farman."

Murdoch looked up from her notebook and our eyes met. She swallowed and licked her lips. Thoughts of those lips being pressed to mine caused my heartrate to increase.

It looked like she was going to say something but instead, she looked away, turned off the recording app and stood up.

Putting her notebook away and returning her phone to her pocket, she said, "Please, keep yourself available for further questions, Ms. Carpenter and that applies to the rest of the ladies, too." "What applies to the rest of the ladies, too?" Harriet was standing in the doorway.

"Nice to see you, Harriet." Murdoch looked from Harriet to me. "I'm sure Ms. Carpenter can bring you up to speed." Murdoch started for the door.

"Wait a minute, detective." My words stopped her. "Beth, Sara, and Tammy all work in Central City. They have jobs to get back to. If you haven't solved this by the end of our weekend, may they be allowed to return to their jobs?"

I could tell Harriet was watching the interaction between the two of us.

Murdoch turned and said, "I'll be able to tell you about Sara and Beth, after I talk to them. But Tammy needs to stay in my jurisdiction until I either clear her or arrest her." Murdoch paused and over her shoulder said, "I have some things to check and then I'll be back. I imagine by then the other ladies will be awake."

The door was just closing on Murdoch when Harriet said, "So, Ms. Carpenter, bring me up to speed."

I flopped into the chair Murdoch had been using. It was still warm from her body heat and smelled like her too. "God what a horrid night."

Harriet sat down opposite me. "Spill."

In a few minutes' time I'd brought Harriet up to speed.

I closed with, "Oh yeah, Tammy is down the hall, and as far as Murdoch needs to know that's where she's been since the beginning."

"Damn girl. I can't leave you unsupervised for one evening without you finding a dead body."

Chuckling, I said, "Yes, well, I have a bone to pick with you, Miss Harriet Walsh."

"What have I done?"

"What was the big idea, giving that Edgar joker my personal information?"

A look of confusion spread over Harriet's face. "I don't know what you're talking about, chère."

"The card reading, there's only one way he could have known the things he was saying to me, and that's if someone told him a great deal about my personal love life."

"Whoa, tiger. I met Edgar for the first-time last night."

Studying Harriet's face, I knew she was telling the truth. "Damn! That's a bit unnerving. How did he…Never mind, just a couple of lucky guesses and some internet research." I shook my head as if that would erase the images I was seeing in my mind. Smiling I asked, "What are you doing up, anyway? This is supposed to be a vacation for you."

Harriet laughed. "I've been getting up so early for so long, it's just habit. Doesn't seem to matter what time I go to bed, I'm up by three, four at the latest."

I yawned and apologized. "Sorry. I haven't been to bed at all."

"That's what I thought. On your feet girl. It's time you got some sleep."

"What about you?"

"I think I'll look in on Amanda and then maybe I'll go back to bed until breakfast."

# CHAPTER 13

The smell of bacon and coffee woke me. I dressed in a fresh polo shirt, slipped the previous day's cargo pants on, and stepped into my walking shoes.

Harriet was already in the dining room, filling her plate.

"Thanks for this little respite from my daily routine, Larissa. It's nice to have someone else do the cooking for a change."

"You deserve a break, now and again." I sighed. "I just wish it wasn't being spoiled by a murder."

Harriet put her plate down and poured some tea for herself.

When I turned from the sideboard, with a full plate of eggs, bacon, fruit, and a pancake I could see Murdoch sitting in her car.

She's either on the phone or talking to herself. Probably running a check on every name involved.

I sat down with my food, put a cloth napkin in my lap, and reached for where a coffee cup should have been. "Crap!" I exhaled heavily.

Harriet was still standing at the sideboard, she looked like she was debating with herself on whether to have a cranberry or a blueberry muffin. She turned from the muffin tray and asked, "What's wrong now, chère?"

I scoffed. "Nothing important, I just forgot to get a cup of coffee." Putting my napkin on the table, I pushed my chair back and started to get up.

"Stay where you are. I'll get you a cup." She poured a cup of coffee and placed it next to my plate. "What you should be drinking is a nice tea, one that would help calm your nerves."

"Thanks." I took a sip of the dark liquid. "Do you really think tea is going to help my situation?"

Harriet glanced out the window at Murdoch. "I suppose not."

Amanda came in from the kitchen. "Good morning, ladies. Is there anything you need?"

Trying to lighten the mood I smiled and asked, "You wouldn't happen to have a time machine lying around, would you?"

"No. Sorry." She checked the buffet on the sideboard. "I'll bring more eggs out."

The fork full of pancake stopped halfway to my mouth when I heard Murdoch's voice.

"Good morning, Ms. Colton."

Amanda turned toward Murdoch and smiled. "Good morning, detective. Please, call me Amanda." She indicated the buffet. "Help yourself. More eggs are on the way."

"Thank you, Amanda." Murdoch grabbed a plate and piled on some eggs, bacon, grabbed a cinnamon muffin, and a cup of coffee.

I pushed the fork into my mouth. Having a mouth full of food prevented me from making any snide remarks.

Murdoch sat down across from me and Harriet. "So, the others haven't come down yet, I see."

Harriet smiled. "We were out rather late last night." She took a sip of her tea and then looking at Murdoch said, "The three of us were at the bar in the Crescent Moon until almost midnight. Then we meandered home." Amanda entered from the kitchen with a fresh batch of scrambled eggs for the buffet.

Harriet spoke to her over her shoulder. "By the way Amanda, thank you so much for the flashlights. Without them we'd have been wandering about until daybreak, trying to find our way back." Harriet turned back to Murdoch. "Do you have any idea how dark it can be at night without a moon? Even with the flashlights, we walked carefully, so I'd say it was close to twelve by the time we got back here." She sipped her tea. "I can't speak for Sara and Beth, but I went to bed and slept like the dead until whatever time it was, I found you in the study."

Realizing what she'd said Harriet apologized. "Sorry, poor choice of words."

Laughter could be heard from the direction of the stairs.

I directed my words to Murdoch, "I do believe you're about to meet Sara and Beth."

Beth's laugh was cut off as she stepped into the dining area and spotted Murdoch. She nodded to Harriet and me and quietly said, "Good morning."

Sara followed her in, nodded to Murdoch in acknowledgement, gave a questioning look at Harriet and me as she too said, "Good morning."

Harriet's melodic voice greeted the two ladies with her good morning.

I tried to smile but it came out as a sigh. "You're half right. It's morning. I'm not sure there's anything good about it."

Murdoch dabbed her mouth with her napkin, placed it next to her plate, and said, "Good morning, ladies. I'm Detective Murdoch of the Hamilton County Sheriff's Department."

"Detective? What's going on here?" Sara directed her query to me.

I exhaled heavily and then drew in a deep breath. "Get yourselves some breakfast, have a seat and I'll tell you all about Tammy and Larissa's Adventures in the Dark of Night in Cerridwen." I glanced at Murdoch. "After breakfast the detective will have a few questions for you both. I doubt that you have anything to worry about." I paused and then unable to control my dark sense of humor said, "Unless of course you killed the witch that lived in the cottage in the woods."

Sara and Beth looked around the room at the others, as if trying to figure out if this was a joke. Realizing that neither of the two ladies, especially Beth, appreciated my humor I continued, "My apologies for trying to lighten the mood. Please, get some breakfast, cup of coffee, and have a seat."

They turned to the buffet, each grabbed a cup of coffee, and a muffin and sat down.

Always the more outgoing of the two, Sara said, "Will someone please tell us what the blazes is going on here?"

All eyes turned to Murdoch. "Do either of you know a woman named Mirabel Fleur?"

The response was a, no, in stereo.

Murdoch went through the process of asking the ladies' permission to record the interview before continuing. They both agreed.

"After leaving the restaurant last night tell me about the rest of the evening."

"Sure." Sara said. "We wandered around town for a bit. Ended up at Edgar's shop. He did some kind of reading on Larissa while the rest of us browsed."

Beth added. "Yeah, and then when Larissa came out of the back-room Edgar was in a real hurry to get us all out of there."

"Yeah, it was really kind of strange." Sara added. "Then Harriet, Beth, and I went to the bar at the Crescent Moon. We got back here, I don't know sometime around midnight, I guess."

"Yeah, it'd been a long day. I think I was asleep before my head hit the pillow."

"Yes, you were." Sara said and with a gentle smile added, "And you snore."

"What?"

Sara laughed. "Just a little, soft snore." Then she grew serious and turned from Beth to Murdoch. "Okay, we've answered your questions. Now is someone going to tell us what this is all about?"

"Mirabel Fleur was found dead by Tammy and Larissa. Before you start asking questions I can't answer. I'll tell you what I can." Murdoch paused. "We don't yet have a cause or a time of death. We're treating it as suspicious, until we know more."

Amanda was straightening the buffet when Cassandra entered from the kitchen. "What's going on?" Her eyes scanned the faces of everyone at the table. Then she turned to her mother. "Mom, why is Det. Murdoch here?"

"Excuse me folks, I need to speak with my daughter." Amanda and Cassandra went into the kitchen.

Now how did Cassandra know Murdoch on sight? Hmmm. That's a question I'll have to ask one of them sometime.

An awkward silence filled the dining room. The only sound was the occasional clink of utensils on plates.

Cassandra's voice carried from the kitchen. "No. That can't be. I saw her just yesterday. She was fine."

Silent tears were running down her face when the young woman returned to the dining room. Looking around the room she demanded, "What about Sasha? Where is she?"

"Sasha? Who is Sasha?" Murdoch asked.

Amanda returned to the dining room behind her daughter. She cleared her throat and answered. "Sasha is Mirabel's cat."

Murdoch looked at me. "Did you see a cat?"

"No, I didn't."

"What does Sasha look like?"

Amanda chuckled. "Exactly like you would expect a witch's cat to look. She's all black."

"Is she strictly an indoor cat?"

"No but the only time she goes outside is when she's with Mirabel. Or if Cassandra's taking care of her, she'll go outside with her. But she never strays. She always stays in the yard."

Amanda drew her daughter into a hug, then held her at arm's length and as if answering a question she said, "Yes, if the detective says it's okay, you may go to Mirabel's and look for Sasha." She slid her glasses to the top of her head, wiped the tears from her face, and kissed her daughter on the forehead before returning to the kitchen.

# CHAPTER 14

Murdoch, Cassandra, and Larissa left the dining room. They went out the back door to the garden. Larissa led the way through the garden to the gate.

Traveling down the dirt road in the light of day was very different than following Tammy to an unknown destination in the middle of a dark night.

In the light of day, her fears of the previous night seemed silly. There was nothing forbidding or spooky about the area. It was simply a one lane dirt road that ran behind the manor to the back of the shops on Ravens Road. The sun was up and shone through the tree branches, creating a beautiful pattern of light and shadow. This time she made certain to stay away from the Bougainvillea.

Larissa could hear Murdoch and Cassandra's voices a little way behind her but was unable to make out the words of the conversation.

Wonder what those two are talking about? Murdoch's probably grilling the poor kid about Mirabel.

Cassandra watched the way Murdoch looked at Larissa for several minutes before asking, "Why haven't you told her how you feel?"

Murdoch stopped and looked at the teenager. "What are you talking about?"

She smiled at the detective. "You're crazy about her" she nodded in Larissa's direction "but you haven't let her know. Why?"

Murdoch began walking again. "It's complicated."

Cassandra laughed softly and shook her head. "That's what adults say when they either don't know the answer, think it's beyond my years to understand, or they're scared. Which is it with you, Det. Murdoch?"

Before Murdoch could reply Cassandra smiled and raced ahead, quickly catching up to Larissa. She glanced back at Murdoch, leaned in close to Larissa and said, "I bet you five dollars I can make the detective race up here."

"How do you plan on doing that?" Larissa asked as she glanced over her shoulder.

"Do we have a bet?"

"Sure."

"Okay. When I finish speaking to you, I want you to look back at the detective, and then look at me in disbelief."

"Sure." Larissa looked over her shoulder at Murdoch and then looked at Cassandra with what she hoped was an expression of disbelief.

In a matter of seconds, Murdoch was in front of Larissa walking backwards. She looked at Cassandra suspiciously, cleared her throat and looking at Larissa, asked, "What are you two talking about?"

Larissa looked at Cassandra, smiled and shook her head. What were those two talking about that made Murdoch feel the need to run up here?

"Nothing important. Just chit chat."

"What's that on your arm?" Murdoch was looking at Larissa's arm.

Larissa looked down at the arm. She hadn't realized the sleeves on this shirt were a little shorter than the one she'd had on earlier. "Oh, that's just a scratch I got last night from the Bougainvillea. The one we passed a little way back."

"Hmm. You should have it looked at or at least put something on it. You wouldn't want it to get infected."

Larissa shrugged. "I'll deal with it later."

Murdoch turned around and fell in beside Cassandra.

"Cassandra, back at the manor you recognized Det. Murdoch. How did you already know her?"

"She was here last year investigating a case." Smiling, Cassandra shrugged. "I just remember her from then."

The rest of the walk was conducted in silence.

# CHAPTER 15

As the trio stood at the edge of Mirabel's yard, there was an air of abandonment about the place. The garden looked sad and in need of care. Already weeds were beginning to take over the soil between plants.

Cassandra sighed heavily and started across the yard.

"Wait."

She stopped and turned to face Murdoch, who said, "Let me check the house first."

While Larissa and Cassandra waited in the garden for Murdoch to check out the house, Larissa pulled out a five-dollar bill and handed it to Cassandra.

Cassandra smiled. She thought Larissa was a good person and she was pleased to find that her judgement was correct.

Murdoch stepped out of the cottage and said, "All clear."

Murdoch and Larissa followed Cassandra in and watched as she stopped at the end of the island and stared at the floor for a moment. She looked at the two adults and said, "This is where she was found." It was a statement, not a question.

Murdoch narrowed her eyes a bit and asked, "How do you know that, Cassandra?"

She tilted her head a bit and gave a small sigh. "I don't know." She shrugged. "I just felt her presence there."

Murdoch watched her walk around the island and step past where Mirabel's body had been. The way Cassandra stepped around the island Murdoch knew that if the body had still been there the girl wouldn't have touched it.

Facing the pantry, just past where Mirabel had lain Cassandra stopped. A slow smile spread over the girl's face. She looked up at the top of the pantry. "Sasha come."

Out of the corner of her eye Larissa caught movement of something close to the ceiling. Across the room a triangular shaped head peeked over the edge of the pantry. The cat's green eyes studied the humans below it.

Cassandra stepped to the other side of the island and said, "Come on down, Sasha. It's safe. No one will hurt you."

As if she understood, the cat gracefully leapt from the top of the pantry to the island, landing next to Cassandra who began petting her. The cat pushed against the girl and then rose on its hind legs, placing its front paws on Cassandra's chest.

"Yes, I know sweetheart. Come on. Let's go home." With that statement the cat climbed up on her shoulders and draped itself around her neck.

Watching Cassandra with Sasha, made Larissa think of Tut and she wondered how he was doing with Vera. She shook her head. I'm sure he's fine. He loves Vera, almost as much as he loves me.

Cassandra opened a drawer in the kitchen island and removed a harness and leash.

Murdoch considered objecting to items being removed from the crime scene and then decided to let it go.

On the walk back to the manor Murdoch asked Cassandra, "Do you know if Mirabel had any family?"

"The coven was her family." She paused. "If you mean, did she have any blood relatives, none that I ever heard her mention."

"What about friends, lovers, boyfriends, girlfriends?"

Cassandra paused for several heartbeats before answering, "I know she and Molly were friends. I think Molly wanted to be more than a friend. I don't think Mirabel was interested in Molly that way. My mother might know more about that."

"I noticed there were a lot of herbs in Mirabel's garden and in the cottage, there were dried herbs. Could she have accidentally poisoned herself?"

Cassandra laughed. "Hardly. Mirabel was a Certified Herbalist. She was teaching Molly and me about plants and herbs. She had probably forgotten more about herbs than the rest of us will ever know." Her face sad, she looked at Murdoch. "I'll miss her."

"Have you seen Molly since your last lesson?"

"Molly and I didn't have lessons at the same time." Rubbing the cat's head absentmindedly, she continued. "We were at different levels."

"You mentioned earlier that you saw Mirabel yesterday. When was that?"

"In the morning probably around ten."

"You didn't see her after that?"

"Hmm. No. I was around the manor, here and there, getting things ready for the arrival of our guests."

"Do you know when Molly's last session with Mirabel was?"

"Uh, actually, I believe it was yesterday afternoon."

"Hmm. What's Molly's last name?"

"I'm not sure. I don't know that I've ever heard it but she's Edgar's sister and his last name is Kerry."

"Do you know where Molly lives?"

"Not really. I mean I know she lives here in Cerridwen. The only time I saw her was when I was at Mirabel's or if she was working a shift at The Cauldron. Maybe she lives with her brother."

"Thank you, Cassandra. You've been a big help."

# CHAPTER 16

Cassandra took the cat to her room, which was across the hall from her mother's room. I returned to the dining room, grabbed a muffin, and another cup of coffee. Murdoch had excused herself and gone back to her car

Just as I was finishing my second cup of coffee, a patrol car pulled up next to Murdoch's car. Expecting Deputy Brighton to emerge from the vehicle, I was surprised when instead a female deputy I'd never seen stepped out.

She stood about five feet six inches, one hundred twenty-five pounds, short hair, and a complexion that looked like honey. The short hair and masculine uniform made my gaydar go off.

I could feel Harriet watching me watch the new arrival. She nodded toward the female deputy and said, "Looks like Murdoch's got a new sidekick."

I took a breath and exhaled sharply. "Let's hope she's got more on the ball than Brighton." Brighton was okay but I think he became a cop in a beach town so he could surf.

Downing the last swallow of my coffee I pushed my chair back, picked up my cup and plate, and took them to the kitchen.

From a small round table on the other side of the kitchen, Amanda said, "You didn't need to do that. One of us will clear the table when everyone's finished with breakfast."

"Yes, I know. I just wanted to get out of there without being asked where I was going."

Amanda nodded and smiled.

Rather than return to the dining room I crossed the kitchen and left by the exit near the stairs and headed upstairs. Remembering that the third step tended to squeak, I avoided it.

Once in my room I stripped and took a shower. I towel dried my hair and gave it a few strokes with a brush. Stepping out of the bathroom, I was glad that I had decided to have Tammy in a room of her own.

I really have become accustomed to being on my own. I enjoy my privacy. Though there are times when… No! Stop it! Getting involved with Murdoch would create complications. Hell, being involved with Tammy has created complications. Enough!

Refreshed and clean, I dressed in a polo shirt, fresh cargo pants, and my walking shoes. I opened the door to the hallway and listened. I couldn't make out what was being said but it was enough to tell me there were still people downstairs.

Most likely Murdoch and her new sidekick. Think I'll leave the back way.

Without the need to worry about tripping a security light or falling over something in the dark, I moved across the garden and out the gate in a matter of seconds.

Ten minutes later I was in downtown Cerridwen. It was only a bit after nine, so most of the shops were still closed.

81

However, The Cauldron was open and though I'd already had breakfast I was always up for another cup of coffee.

Standing just inside the door I decided that sitting at the bar might be more advantageous than occupying a table. I chose the stool closest to the register.

"Good morning, ma'am. What can I get for you?"

"Good morning, Sybil. I'll start with coffee, black."

At first Sybil seemed taken aback that I knew her name, then she recognized me.

"Where's the rest of your crew?" She asked, smiling. "They decide to sleep in?"

I chuckled and sipped my coffee. "The elixir of life. You make good coffee."

"Thanks." Sybil was a natural at customer service and knew how to draw people into conversations. "So, you and your friends in town for a girl's weekend?"

"Yes. We'd all heard a great deal about Cerridwen and decided it would be fun to come and see what it's all about."

Leaning in and keeping my voice low I asked, "Are there any real psychics or witches here?" Sybil looked at me questioningly. "No. I'm serious. I'm not making fun or joking."

Sybil studied me for a moment or two, then looked around as if she were checking to see if there was anyone close enough to overhear. Then she stepped closer to the counter. "I don't know what you've heard but some of these people take what they do very seriously."

"Good. That's what I'm looking for." I paused. "What about Edgar? He gave me a reading last night, well, actually he only gave me part of a reading. It was like he saw something that spooked him, and he kicked all of us out of his shop."

82

"Yeah, Edgar's the real deal. He can give you a reading or" she looked around again "I've heard if he touches you, he can see your future."

"Seriously." I went back in my mind to when Edgar had brushed against my hand. Yep, that's when he got spooked. Oh bullshit. I don't believe in this nonsense.

"Well, not the details but he gets an impression of things to come. You know, love, death, extreme wealth, stuff like that."

"Excellent. I'll have to make sure I go see him again." I sipped my coffee, wondering how far Sybil would go in confiding in me. "I need some herbs. Is there anybody around here that sells the real stuff? I mean I can order things online, but you just never know what you're really getting. I don't live that far away and driving over here to pick things up is no big deal."

"Yeah. There's a cottage beyond the woods, that are behind the parking lot." She nodded her head toward the back of the restaurant. Just go through the parking lot back there, behind the hedge you'll see a path. Just follow that and you'll end up at Mirabel's. She has a degree in botany, and she grows all of her own stuff."

Sybil checked the time. "As a matter of fact, she should be here by now. She's supposed to be working the morning shift today. Waiting tables, bussing, whatever needs doing." A frown creased Sybil's face. "And until today, she's never been late. The tourists will start showing up in the next little bit, not to mention the locals, and I'm going to need her."

I took a large swallow of my coffee before carefully placing the cup in the center of its saucer. "Sybil, I'm sorry to be the one to tell you, but Mirabel is dead."

"What?!?"

In the antique mirror on the wall behind Sybil, I saw Murdoch enter. Behind her was the uniformed deputy, I'd seen back at the manor.

Murdoch's gold detective's shield hung around her neck on a lanyard. Sybil looked from Murdoch to me and back to Murdoch. "Is it true?"

"Is what true, ma'am?"

"That Mirabel's dead."

Murdoch gave me a scorching look. She softened her features before turning her eyes to Sybil. "Yes, ma'am. I'm afraid it is true. I'm Detective Murdoch. This is Deputy Santos. We'll be investigating Ms. Fleur's death. And you are?"

"Investigating? Does that mean she was murdered?"

"The cause of death hasn't been determined. In such situations, we treat the death as suspicious." She glanced at me. "Is there somewhere private we can talk, Ms…?"

"Sorry. I'm Sybil Morton." She looked around the dining room at the few early risers, that she'd already seated and served. "And no, I can't go wandering off for a private conversation. I'll have to do my job and Mirabel's." She pursed her lips. "This is our busiest time of year."

In a calm voice, I offered, "Sybil, it'll be okay. I've worked in a restaurant before. Granted it's been a few years, but I think I remember how to seat people, take their orders, and if need be, even run a cash register."

I smiled at Murdoch. "Ask the detective about my trustworthiness."

Murdoch raised an eyebrow and gave a partial smile to Sybil. "Yes, I guarantee Ms. Carpenter's honesty. She won't steal from the till." She paused. "As for her skills as a waitress, I have no doubt that if she says she can do it, she can."

Sybil straightened her posture, which had sagged upon hearing about Mirabel. "Thank you, Ms. Carpenter. I accept your offer of help." She looked past me to the front door. "There's a couple coming in now. If you would be so kind as to take care of them, I would appreciate it."

"Done." I moved to the door and greeted the couple.

# CHAPTER 17

Sybil looked at Murdoch. "This is as private as a conversation with me is going to get until after closing, detective."

"What can you tell me about Mirabel Fleur?"

Sybil removed Larissa's coffee cup and put it on the shelf of the pass through. "Not much. Her help here in the restaurant will be missed." She watched Larissa working the dining room before bringing her attention back to Murdoch. A soft smile turned her lips up. "Oh yeah, and I suppose I will have to find a new provider for the herbs she grew."

"Herbs?"

"Yes, we use fresh Rosemary and Basil in some of our recipes. I'm sure that Chef knows more about that than I do." She half-smiled. "I don't know the recipes that well."

"Can you think of anyone who would want to harm Ms. Fleur?"

"No. Mirabel was liked by everyone."

"No recent arguments, squabbles, or falling out between friends?"

"Not that I know of."

"What about Molly Kerry?"

Sybil stopped wiping down the counter and looked at Murdoch. "What does Molly have to do with this?"

In an attempt to put Sybil at ease, Murdoch smiled and said, "I need to talk to everyone who knew Ms. Fleur. I understand that she was taking herbology classes from Ms. Fleur."

Sybil chuckled. "Let me give a piece of advice detective. When you ask people about her, call her Mirabel. Most people around here won't know who you're talking about, calling her Ms. Fleur."

"I'll keep that in mind. Now about Molly."

"Yes, Molly was taking classes from Mirabel. That girl would have stood on her head and spit wooden nickels if Mirabel asked her to."

"Hmm. What about her brother, Edgar?"

"What about him?"

"Did he object to Molly's relationship with Mirabel?"

"There was no relationship to object to. I don't think Mirabel was even aware of Molly's feelings toward her."

"Can you tell me where Molly lives?"

"With her brother Edgar. They've got one of the apartments behind the shops. Not sure which building. Might be to the south or maybe north of the parking lot."

"What exactly does Edgar do? I know that your new waitress" she indicated Larissa "and her friends went to see him after they left here last night." Studying Sybil intently she continued. "Something happened during a reading he was giving, and he chased them out of his shop."

Laughing, Sybil said, "Oh that, that's just a ploy Edgar uses to get people curious about what he saw. When they come back, they're begging him to tell them what it was he saw."

Throughout the interview Sybil kept looking away from Murdoch. Her refusal to look Murdoch in the eye, made the detective doubt her truthfulness.

"Hmmm." Murdoch scribbled in her notebook.

While the detective was talking with Sybil a few more customers entered The Cauldron. Soon Larissa was clipping orders to the old-fashioned order wheel ticket holder, filling, and delivering coffee cups, and glasses of juice.

Sybil's attention was divided between her conversation with Murdoch and watching Larissa.

A family of five, two adults and three rowdy children came in, Sybil looked at Murdoch and said, "If there's nothing else, I really do need to get back to work."

Murdoch glanced back at the dining area. "Yes, that's all for now and I do believe Ms. Carpenter could use your help." She leaned toward Sybil and quietly added, "She's not real fond of children, especially ill-mannered ones."

# CHAPTER 18

Sitting in Santos' patrol car outside The Cauldron, Murdoch reviewed the notes she had so far.

Santos asked, "Where to boss?"

Murdoch looked up and down the street. It was almost ten and the shops would all be open soon.

"I'll walk back to the manor from here. I want you to go to the station and do some research. I want background info on everyone we've talked to, except for Larissa Carpenter and Harriet Walsh. Don't waste time on them."

Santos looked confused. "Why not those two?"

Murdoch turned in her seat so that she was facing Santos. She studied the younger woman for a few moments. "Don't play stupid, Santos. It doesn't look good on you."

Returning to her notes she continued, "I want to know everything about Mirabel Fleur, who owns The Cauldron. Who owns Mirabel's cottage and who are Edgar Kerry and his sister, Molly?" She paused. "While you're at it find out everything you can about Sybil Morton and Tammy Lopez?"

"What about the other ladies?"

"Hmmm. Yeah, do backgrounds on Sara and Beth too. But I'm not nearly as interested in them as the others, especially Lopez."

89

"What about Amanda Colton and her daughter?"

"No. I already did a background on them not that long ago. Another case."

Murdoch opened the car door, leaned back in and added, "Oh yeah, and find me a history of this town. From its founding forward."

"Where will you be?"

Smiling Murdoch said, "Right now I'm going to talk to Edgar Kerry, among others. Eventually, I'll be back at the manor."

Standing on the sidewalk, Murdoch watched Santos drive out of town. She could feel the eyes of many people watching her. Word had spread quickly about Mirabel's death.

While Murdoch was giving Santos her marching orders, The Cauldron became a beehive of activity. Between customers coming in the front door and locals sliding in through the kitchen Larissa and Sybil were kept hopping.

Edgar Kerry entered The Cauldron through the kitchen. Looking into the dining room to see if Molly was working, he saw Larissa waiting tables. His eyes narrowed, nostrils flared, and as Sybil started past him, he grabbed her arm.

Pointing toward Larissa he demanded, "What is she doing here? I told Tammy last night, that death follows that one. Now Mirabel is dead."

Sybil looked into Edgar's eyes and calmly said, "Either let go of me or I'll knee you in the nuts so hard they'll pop out of your nose."

Edgar released her arm and stormed out the front door.

Sybil stood staring after him.

On her way to put in an order Larissa passed by Sybil. "What was he on about?"

Sybil looked at her with a mischievous grin and said, "Something about you being a harbinger of death." Then she turned and entered the kitchen.

Larissa spun toward the windows that looked out on the street. On the sidewalk, Murdoch was talking with Edgar.

Murdoch's expression was blank, but it was obvious that Edgar was agitated. She watched Murdoch move into the man's personal space. Her thoughts were interrupted by the cook calling. "Order up."

Larissa grabbed the order and had to stop and study it for several seconds before it dawned on her which table it belonged to.

Guess I'll have to pay more attention to my job and put the murder investigation on the back burner.

# CHAPTER 19

Murdoch followed Edgar into his shop. She took in the crystals and herbs at a glance and spotted the curtain that separated the private reading room. On the wall to her right was a small selection of books on the paranormal, herbology, and witchcraft.

"What can you tell me about Mirabel?"

Edgar moved around the store straightening items on shelves and rearranging things as he spoke. "Not much. She was well-liked. I can't think of anyone who would want to harm her." He sniffed some of the hanging herbs behind the counter. "I can give you a good deal on these, they won't stay viable much longer. Hmmm. I suppose I'll have to find my herbs somewhere else now that Mirabel's crossed over."

"You're the second person to mention that Mirabel supplied them with herbs." She paused but Edgar didn't say anything. "I understand that Mirabel was teaching your sister Molly about herbs. Can you tell me where I can find Molly? I'd like to talk to her."

Edgar looked at Murdoch in alarm. "Why? She didn't have anything to do with Mirabel's death."

Murdoch's face remained expressionless. "I'm talking to everyone who was close to Mirabel. Anyone who knew or came in contact with her might have information vital to my investigation." She smiled. "They may not even know that what they heard, or saw was important." She paused. "So, about your sister Molly?"

"Molly's a free spirit. Sometimes she stays at my place, but she wasn't there last night. Probably with one of the" his next words were said with disdain "Cerridwen Coven."

"The Cerridwen Coven?"

Edgar almost smiled. "Yes. Molly fancies herself a witch. She belongs to the local coven. Sometimes she stays with one of the other witches." He grabbed a sprayer of glass cleaner and wiped down the countertop. "Thankfully she didn't spend last night at Mirabel's."

"Where does she work?"

"Here and there. Like I said, she's a…"

"Yeah, a free spirit."

"Although with The Cauldron being shorthanded, Sybil may have called her to come in."

"What's her phone number?"

Edgar mentally kicked himself. Damn it! Now Molly'll be pissed at me for giving a cop her phone number.

"Well, I'm not sure it's still in service. She's not really good about keeping up with her bills."

"Mr. Kerry, you can either give me your sisters phone number or we can go to the station for a more in-depth interview, which could take hours."

"I have a business to run, and this is my busy season."

"It's up to you."

Edgar grabbed a pad from the shelf under the register, wrote Molly's phone number down, tore out the page and handed it to Murdoch.

"Thank you, Mr. Kerry. I'm sure we'll be talking again." Murdoch started for the door.

"The one you should be talking to is that woman at The Cauldron. That Larissa Carpenter."

She stopped and turned back to Edgar. "Oh, why is that?"

Edgar smoothed his mustache and pulled himself up to his full five feet eleven inches. "I saw it last night. My hand brushed hers during the card reading. Death and danger are all around that woman."

"Hmmm. Thanks. I'll keep that in mind." She turned to leave.

"Scoff if you wish but you mark my words, that one is dangerous."

Murdoch waved goodbye and thought to herself, "You have no idea, how right you are."

# CHAPTER 20

The breakfast rush was over. There was only one couple left in the dining room, sipping coffee, and looking longingly into each other's eyes.

Larissa sat down at the counter.

Sybil was behind the counter filling sugar bowls.

Larissa stretched, rubbed her lower back, and said, "I'd forgotten what hard work being nice to people can be."

Sybil chuckled. "I appreciate you helping out. There was no way I could have managed this morning, without your help."

"Order up." A plate with a pile of scrambled eggs, a pancake, and a couple of slices of bacon appeared on the shelf under the ticket wheel.

"I don't remember putting in that order." Larissa looked around the room. The last couple in the dining room was just leaving and there was no one at the counter with her.

Sybil placed the plate in front of Larissa. "Interested in second breakfast?" she asked as she put a cup of coffee on the counter next to the plate.

Larissa smiled. "Thank you." Her stomach growled. "Yes, I hadn't realized how hungry I was until now."

In between refilling condiment containers Sybil kept Larissa's coffee cup full.

When Larissa finished her meal and pushed the plate back, she asked, "What will you do about lunch and dinner? Cause as much as I've enjoyed spending time here, I'm not looking for a job."

Sybil laughed. "Molly will be here for the lunch rush, until then I can manage. I'll see if I can get her to hang around and help Donna with the dinner crowd. If not her" she shrugged "maybe Cassandra would like to earn a few dollars."

Larissa perked up at the mention of Molly's name. "Molly, she's Edgar's sister, right?"

"Yeah." Sybil looked up from her work. "How did you know that?"

Larissa smiled. "I've just spent the last couple of hours talking to a lot of people. Some of them locals that Edgar hasn't poisoned with the idea that I'm a harbinger of death."

She pulled her tip money from the pocket of the apron she'd been wearing and counted close to thirty dollars. Leaving the money on the counter next to the apron, Larissa asked, "Did Mirabel have a favorite charity?"

Sybil thought for a moment. "Yes, there's an animal rescue place that she used to talk about. Whether she donated money, her time, or both, I don't know. I think it was called Journey's End."

"Excellent! My tips and whatever other money I earned here today can be donated to them in Mirabel's name."

"That's very generous of you. You didn't even know Mirabel."

"No, but Tammy did." Larissa swallowed the last of her coffee and stood up. "I'm sure the ladies and I will be in for lunch today." She headed for the door and over her should said, "See you around, Sybil."

Standing on the sidewalk Larissa surveyed the activity on the street. Tourists popping in and out of shops, shopkeepers talking with customers, and the occasional sound of laughter. If she didn't know about the murder, she would think it was just a day like any other in Cerridwen.

It was a cool eighty degrees. Larissa decided to travel the back way to Ravenswood Manor. She enjoyed the dappled patterns made by the old oaks draped in Spanish Moss that formed a canopy over the dirt road leading to the manor's garden.

Reviewing all the facts she had at her disposal and a few conjectures, she was lost in thought and walked right past the back gate to Ravenswood's garden before she realized where she was.

She walked the few feet back to the garden gate and entered. Halfway across the garden she stopped and looked back at the gate.

It didn't squeak. Hmmm. Wonder who oiled it and why?

Instead of climbing the back stairs to her room, Larissa walked around to the front of the house and entered through the front door. Just inside the entry way were two bags.

She heard voices coming from the living room to her left. Murdoch was talking with Sara and Beth.

"Thank you for your cooperation. I've got your contact information if I have any other questions."

Sara saw Larissa enter the room. "We were waiting for you. We're headed home."

"Sorry things turned out like this. I was hoping for a nice quiet and relaxing weekend for all of us."

Beth wouldn't meet Larissa's gaze and Sara looked nervous. Larissa looked from Beth to Murdoch to Sara. "Has something else happened?"

Sara was too quick to respond. "No. I'll call you. Stay safe, Larissa."

Sara and Beth were gone before Larissa could think of anything else to say. She turned to Murdoch. "Can you tell me what that was all about?"

Murdoch rubbed the back of her neck and walked to the picture window that looked out on the driveway. She watched the two women load their car as she said, "I really think you should ask your friend Sara."

"I'm asking you."

Murdoch turned to face her, as she opened her mouth to speak, Tammy came into the room.

"Where've you been all morning, love?"

Despite the fact that she was annoyed with Tammy for spoiling the weekend by finding the dead body of her ex-lover, she smiled.

A quick glance at Murdoch confirmed what she already knew, Murdoch didn't like Tammy.

Hmmm. I wonder if that's just because she suspects her of murder or because she called me love. I wonder if she thinks we're sleeping together.

Larissa chuckled and Murdoch asked, "What's so funny?"

"Nothing." She looked at Tammy and said, "I've been working at The Cauldron."

"What?"

Larissa snapped, "What part of that sentence was confusing to you?" Tammy's face flushed, but before she could respond, "Sorry, Tammy. I'm just frustrated and tired." Larissa flopped into a chair.

Tammy rolled her head around on her shoulders, sighed and sat down opposite Larissa. "Yeah. It's a bit of a cock-up, for sure."

Murdoch moved in and sat down where she could see both women. She put her phone on the end table next to her. "Is it all right to record this conversation? It really helps me later." She smiled. "I don't want to rely on my memory for something this important."

"No problem."

Tammy nodded her agreement.

Murdoch said, "Ms. Lopez, I need your agreement verbally."

"Sure. Whatever."

"Thank you." Murdoch paused, thinking about how best to phrase her question. "I, uh, I've talked to a lot of people in town. Seems that Mirabel was well-liked. Is it possible that she accidentally poisoned herself?"

Tammy shook her head vigorously. "No! No way! That woman knew every plant in existence and some that are extinct. No way this was an accident."

Holding Tammy's gaze Murdoch, gently asked, "Suicide?"

"Ha. There's less chance of that than of an accident."

Murdoch continued to study Tammy as she leaned back in her chair and asked, "Then who would want to kill her?"

99

"Buggered if I know." Tammy jumped up from her chair and began furiously pacing the room.

Murdoch let her blow off some steam before she said, "Please, sit back down, Ms. Lopez."

Tammy looked at her as if she wanted to strangle her. Then she exhaled sharply and returned to her chair.

"Let's attack this from a different angle. Tell me about Mirabel. Her likes, dislikes, habits, anything that comes to mind. It helps me to know the victim. How did you two meet?"

Tammy looked from Larissa to Murdoch, sighed and leaned back in her chair. "I met Mirabel when I joined the local coven." She studied Larissa for signs of a reaction but didn't see any.

I did tell her I'm a witch, still there's a bit of difference between someone telling you they're a witch and learning they belonged to a coven.

"That was, three, no four years ago. Right here in Cerridwen. We became lovers and things were great for a while, but I've never been much of a joiner. I left the coven." She smiled. "Don't get me wrong, I'm still a practicing witch." She shrugged. "I just don't belong to a coven."

Murdoch studied Tammy for a moment, before taking a deep breath and saying, "I don't want to offend you; however, what exactly does that mean?"

Tammy knew what the detective was asking; however, she decided to play with the her a bit. "What does what mean?"

"What does it mean that you're a practicing witch?"

"Seeking knowledge isn't offensive. There are a variety of practicing witches. First, let me assure you I don't eat children,

100

or sacrifice virgins. The virgin thing is mostly because they're really hard to find."

Murdoch almost smiled at Tammy's attempt at humor.

"Basically, I make charms, cast spells, and observe all the appropriate holidays."

"I find this a fascinating topic, but I don't think it's particularly relevant to the investigation, so I'll move on to other things."

"When you want to know more feel free to ask."

"Thank you. How did Mirabel feel about you leaving the coven?"

"Leaving the coven wasn't a problem. Wanting to leave Cerridwen was a problem. She loved her little cottage in the woods with all her plants. Mirabel was definitely a Garden Witch. I wanted to live in a city." She sighed. "We agreed to disagree. I left for Central City, and she stayed here."

"When did you last see her?"

"That's been a while. I'd say I've been gone from Cerridwen about, a year. But we'd ring each other now and again." She paused. "Let's see I think the last time she rang me was about two, three days ago." Tammy smiled. "It was hard not to tell her I was coming here for the weekend. I wanted to surprise her. Mirabel loved surprises."

"What did you two talk about on that last call?"

"Stuff." She shrugged. "Nothing important. She was telling me about her students. Mirabel loved teaching about plants." She sniffled. "Cassandra's a quick study. Mirabel told me that Cassandra was a natural. Seems she understands plants the way some people grasp technology."

Larissa asked, "What about Molly?

Tammy chuckled. "Seems Molly had a bit of a crush on Mirabel. How did Mirabel put it?" She paused as she dredged up the memory. "Oh yeah, she said if Molly spent as much time on learning as she does on trying to curry my favor, she'd already be an herbalist."

Murdoch moved forward on her chair. "Tell me about Mirabel's habits. What was her daily routine?"

Tammy tilted her head back and looked up at the ceiling. "Get up around six, deal with toiletries, feed Sasha…" She brought her gaze back to Murdoch. "By the way, has anyone taken care of Sasha?"

Larissa smiled. "Yes, Cassandra has her."

Tammy smiled. "Good. Cass and the cat always did get along. Breakfast was usually tea and oatmeal. Then she'd meditate. Water those plants that needed it. Spend some time in the garden doing this and that. I think she taught Cassandra in the morning. At two she would fix a smoothie, put the blender jar in the sink to soak. Then it was back out to the garden, maybe go for a walk in the woods. I think Molly's instruction was in the afternoon, probably around three. Dinner was usually a salad, occasionally she'd have a bit of meat with it but mostly her protein came from the powder that went into her smoothie. Wash up the dishes, read, and…"

"Did she always leave the blender jar in the sink?"

"Well, yeah. Breakfast dishes, blender jar, all sat in the sink until after dinner. Then she washed them all and put them on the dish rack to dry."

"What time did she normally have dinner?"

"Sixish."

It would have been getting dark by six. She'd have turned on lights.

"Were there lights on when you got to the cottage?"

"No." Larissa interjected. "I was about 20 feet from the trailhead when I saw the lights come on."

"Hmmm. Once the dishes were dry did she put them away?"

"No." A faint smile touched Tammy's lips. "I asked her once why she never put the dishes back in the cabinet. She laughed and told me that would be a waste of time and energy." She looked at Larissa. "You know, she was just going to get the same items back out for the next day."

Murdoch looked at Larissa and then back to Tammy. "Did she ever wash things up as she went along?"

"Not in the two years I lived with her. Dishes in the sink until after dinner."

"Did Mirabel have any family?"

"No blood relatives that I know of. The coven was her family."

"Do you know if she had a will?"

Tammy shrugged. "Not sure. Maybe Amanda knows."

"Why would Amanda know?"

"Amanda is the leader of the coven. The last I knew there were no solicitors, or as you call them here, lawyers, in the coven. Mirabel, might have asked Amanda for a recommendation."

"Thank you, Tammy. I appreciate your help." Murdoch turned off the recorder on her phone and stood. "That's all for now. I may have more questions later."

# CHAPTER 21

Tammy went to the garden to be alone, and Murdoch was checking in with Santos. I was delighted to have some alone time, to think.

I got comfortable in one of the wingback chairs, closed my eyes, and went back in my mind to the previous night.

Tammy left the lights on, so the kitchen was fully lit when I entered. I walked around the island and there was Mirabel on the floor. I looked around to see if there was anything remarkable about the place.

In my mind I looked around the kitchen. Bare, clean counters. Empty sink. Empty dishrack. I found a notepad and started scribbling, working out the time frame of events, as I mumbled to myself.

"We found her around midnight. There was no rigor mortis, so she'd been dead less than twelve hours." I looked up and stared blankly out the picture window. "Tammy said Mirabel always left the days dishes until after dinner and there were no dishes in the sink or the dish rack. So, she either died after cleaning up the days dishes or someone cleaned up after she died."

In my mind, I went back over what Tammy had said about Mirabel's daily routine. She said Mirabel never put the dishes away. Whoever killed her didn't know that. That's why there were no dirty dishes in the sink and no clean dishes in the dishrack. Someone washed everything and put it away.

Taking a deep breath, I stood and decided to go find Murdoch. I need to know time of death.

Looking out the dining room window, I could see Murdoch in her car. Either she was talking to herself, or she was on the phone with someone.

Standing next to the car, its windows open I could hear Murdoch's side of the conversation.

"Right. Got it." She paused. "Please, convey my appreciation for the fast autopsy to Dr. Cameron. Any word on that piece of glass or the contents of the trash can? She thinks it's what?" Murdoch wrote something in her notebook. "Seriously. Okay, let me know as soon as we get confirmation on that. Later."

I climbed into the passenger seat of Murdoch's car. "Autopsy results already? Cameron may be a bitch but she's fast."

Murdoch smiled. "Eavesdropping again, Ms. Carpenter?"

"What was time of death?"

Shaking her head in disbelief, Murdoch looked at me. "Why should I tell you? Technically, you're a suspect."

"Okay, since I'm a suspect, what timeframe do I need an alibi for?"

Murdoch laughed. "Where were you between two in the afternoon and six in the evening yesterday?"

"Hmmm. At two, I was going over Tut and Cleo's care with Vera. By three, Harriet and I were on the road, headed here. Traffic was horrid. We arrived right around four thirty and hung around waiting for everyone else to arrive. Tammy showed up between five thirty and six. Around six, we all headed into town for dinner. I'm sure Amanda will confirm that I was here."

I closed my eyes and drew in a long breath of the fall air before saying, "If Mirabel was true to her habit with the dishes, someone cleaned up after she was dead. Someone who wasn't aware of her kitchen habits."

"What makes you say that?" Murdoch was studying me and as I searched her face, I fought the urge to lean across the seat and kiss her.

Instead, I cleared my throat and said, "Since rigor hadn't set in when she was found..."

"How do you know that rigor hadn't set in?"

Shit and damn! I can't tell her I touched the body, even if it was just to lift a finger.

Then I remembered I was there when Murdoch asked Cameron about time of death.

"Remember, I was there when Cameron said rigor was just starting." I shrugged. "That was around four a.m."

She looked at me suspiciously. "Continue."

"I know Cameron's given you a more precise time of death than the four-hour window you asked me about." I studied her for signs that I was correct. She was getting better at maintaining a poker face. "Anyway, I figure the poison was in her two o'clock smoothie and she was dead by four."

"What makes you think she was poisoned?"

I sighed. "There were no outward signs of injury. No blood on the floor. Her neck was visible. No signs of strangulation. If she were smothered with something, like say, a pillow, I doubt her body would have been found in the kitchen. Doesn't leave much beyond poison?"

"You know you have a fascinating way of looking at things. What about natural causes?"

I laughed. "Please, if you thought this was a natural death you wouldn't still be here."

Murdoch rolled her head around on her shoulders and then rubbed the back of her neck. She exhaled sharply. "Yeah, pretty much every organ in her body shut down, though the most damage was to the liver. Nothing natural about that."

"Has Dr. Cameron identified the poison yet?"

Murdoch hesitated, studying me, then said, "Dr. Cameron thinks it's Pennyroyal oil. We're waiting on the lab for confirmation. Ever heard of it?"

"Can't say I have. It sounds like something you'd have to actually be looking for to find. How did Cameron figure it out so quickly?"

"There was a broken glass in the trash. It reeked of mint. Evidently that's a signature of this Pennyroyal oil."

"What are the symptoms? Is there an antidote?"

Murdoch shook her head. "You're a unique person, Ms. Carpenter. She did say it has no antidote and it's a slow, painful death. Once it's been administered, you're done for. The amount administered and the person's health status determine whether it will take hours or days for the victim to die."

"Hmmm. So, someone wanted to make sure she was going to have a painful death."

"Yeah." Murdoch paused. "What's your take on Cameron? I mean, I tried to be friendly and got verbally slapped for my effort."

"She's not afraid to speak her mind."

"No shit, Sherlock." Murdoch went back to reading her notes.

"Have you tried reading her personnel file? Or talking to people that she's worked with before?" I paused and smiled. "Or you could hire a private investigator to do a background check on her?"

Murdoch snorted. "Have you ever considered becoming a cop?"

"Seriously?" I held Murdoch's gaze. "Do you really see me following all the rules and protocols you have to abide by?"

Shaking her head, Murdoch replied, "No, I guess not."

I checked the time. "How about if I take you to The Cauldron for a late lunch?"

# CHAPTER 22

Harriet stepped out of her room, onto the balcony and took a deep breath. It was laden with the scents of fall. The low humidity combined with the wind from the northeast made it almost cool enough for a sweater or light jacket. Almost.

Running My Place was a twenty-four-hour seven day a week job and having this time off was a wonderful break. The problem was that she was so used to being busy that without any demands on her time, she was at a bit of a loss.

Seeing Tammy sitting on the north bench near the center fountain, staring into the water Harriet headed downstairs to the garden.

She stepped up next to Tammy and in her New Orleans patois asked, "Mind if I join you?"

Tammy looked at her and shrugged. From her red eyes and the tear stains on her face, Harriet knew she'd been crying.

"Tell me about Mirabel. What was she like?"

Tammy's voice was filled with suspicion as she asked, "Why?"

"Because it will do you good to talk about her, to tell someone, who doesn't look at you as a murder suspect, about the woman you cared about."

Taking a ragged breath Tammy looked around the garden and said, "She loved plants. She was such a gentle soul." She shook her head. "I just can't imagine anyone wanting to kill her."

"How did you two get together?"

"I'd heard about Cerridwen and visited on my way from up north to Central City." She sniffed. "I literally ran into Mirabel as she was coming out of The Cauldron. I apologized and invited her to have lunch with me." Tammy laughed. "To say I was surprised when she said yes, would be an understatement."

Tammy released a deep sigh. "I feigned an interest in plants and herbs. All I wanted was to be in her presence and that was what she talked about, plants and herbs. That ginger hair and those green eyes. God she was beautiful. She was already a member of the coven." She paused. "I took a room at Ravenswood and became one of Mirabel's students. I learned more about herbs than I ever thought possible." Smiling Tammy looked at Harriet. "She knew from the beginning that the only reason I was interested in herbs and plants, was because I was interested in her."

"How come you two broke up?"

Tammy sighed. "Yeah, that was all me too. I didn't want to live here. Too quiet, no night life to speak of and I wanted to be in a city, where I could earn some real money."

"How did Mirabel make ends meet?"

"She always told me that she didn't really need a lot of money. She inherited the cottage, free and clear." Tammy inhaled deeply. "Selling her organic produce and herbs to The

Cauldron and a couple of other close by restaurants was her main source of income. She sold a few things online."

"So, she has a website?"

"Yes, she does. I wonder if there's anything there that can help the detective." Tammy stood up. "Do you know where Murdoch is?"

Harriet rose. "Not for sure, chère, but let's go find her."

The two women went into the house. Not finding anyone in the living room, Harriet suggested, "Why don't you wait here chère and I'll see if Amanda knows where we can find Murdoch."

A few moments later Harriet came back and found Tammy staring out the front window. "Seems she and Larissa were sitting in Murdoch's car for a while and then they took off toward town, on foot." Harriet looked at her watch. "Probably headed for lunch. You know how that Larissa is, got to be fed every few hours."

Tammy smiled. "Yes, and yet she never seems to gain weight."

"Yes, I'd love to know her secret. All I have to do is look at food and I gain weight. Come on."

"Where are we going?"

"The Cauldron."

"I'm not hungry."

"Doesn't matter, remember, you wanted to talk to Murdoch and she's probably at The Cauldron. Come on, chère, the walk will do you good and you can keep me company while I eat."

Reluctantly, Tammy agreed and followed Harriet.

# CHAPTER 23

As Murdoch and Larissa entered The Cauldron Larissa nodded to Sybil, who was behind the counter wiping it down and clearing dishes.

"Afternoon, detective. Larissa. Seat yourselves. I'll send Molly right over."

Murdoch said, "Afternoon, Ms. Morton."

Sybil stepped into the kitchen where Molly was loading the dishwasher. "Molly."

"Yeah." The girl sounded a bit sullen to Sybil's ear. "Det. Murdoch is here. She wants to talk to you." She watched Molly's eyes dart to the back door. "You're going to have to talk to her sooner or later." She paused. "And she knows you're here."

With an exasperated sigh, Molly dried her hands and headed for the dining room. When Molly went to move past Sybil, Sybil reached out and brushed the girl's hair behind her ear. "You'll be fine."

Molly made a face and moved on.

Sybil watched her leave the kitchen. I'm a poor substitute for Mirabel, but maybe over time…

Shaking her head Sybil finished loading the dishwasher and turned it on.

Standing next to Murdoch and Larissa's table, Molly wore a forced smile, and said, "Good afternoon, my name is Molly. What can I get for you?"

Murdoch stood, flashed her badge, and said, "I'm Detective Murdoch, Molly. I'd like to ask you some questions. Please, sit down."

The smile disappeared and Molly looked around as if trying to decide which way to run. Larissa watched her panic fade as she said, "Sybil doesn't like for us to sit with the customers." No sense in letting her know I was told she was waiting for me.

Murdoch moved to her right and indicated the chair she'd been sitting in. "Please, have a seat. I assure you Sybil won't mind."

Hesitantly, Molly sat down. Murdoch pulled out the chair between Molly and Larissa for herself. She placed her phone on the table and turned on the recording app.

"Interview with Molly…Molly what's your last name?"

"Kerry. Molly Kerry."

"Interview with Molly Kerry regarding the murder of Mirabel Fleur. Molly do I have your permission to record this interview."

Molly nodded her assent.

"Let the record show that Molly Kerry has given non-verbal permission for this interview to be recorded. Also present is Larissa Carpenter. Ms. Carpenter, do I have your permission to record your participation in this interview?"

"Yes."

"Thank you."

"Why didn't you show up for your lesson with Mirabel yesterday afternoon?" Molly was slow to answer, and Murdoch pushed the issue. "And if you did show up, why didn't you report Mirabel's death?"

Keeping her face expressionless Molly said, "I phoned Mirabel earlier in the day to tell her I wouldn't be there. I had some personal business to attend to."

"Hmmm. What was this business that prevented you're attendance?"

"As I said, it was personal."

"Molly this is a murder investigation. Where were you yesterday between two in the afternoon and six in the evening?"

Molly looked down at her clasped hands in her lap, then brought her eyes back up. She briefly met Murdoch's gaze and then moved her eyes to look over Murdoch's left shoulder. "I was passed out. I had started drinking earlier in the day. Once I realized I'd had too much to drink, I, uh, I called Mirabel." She smiled thinly. "Told her I wasn't feeling well, and I wouldn't be in for class."

"Do you normally drink to excess?"

"No."

"What prompted this bout of excessive drinking? I mean, if it's not normal for you to get drunk, then there must have been a reason. What was that reason?"

Larissa watched Molly's reactions to Murdoch's questions.

"What difference does it make? I told you where I was. Are we finished here? I have work to do, to get ready for the dinner crowd."

Larissa jumped in before Murdoch could answer Molly. "What's your favorite drink, Molly?"

"I don't know whiskey, I suppose."

"Which one? People who don't drink often have a favorite for when they do like to drink. Personally, I prefer The Dorak's Whiskey."

Molly smiled and looking directly at Murdoch said, "Yes, that's the one I was drinking the other day, The Dorak's Whiskey."

"Hmmm. That'll be all for now, Ms. Kerry. Don't leave town, I'm certain I'll have more questions." She turned off the recorder and pocketed her phone.

Molly made a quick exit to the kitchen. Glaring at Sybil she said, "I'm taking a break. I'll be back for the dinner crowd."

Sybil watched her storm out the back door. Then she moved to the door and opened it a crack. She watched Molly enter her brother's shop through its back door.

Larissa studied Murdoch and said, "You know she's lying. There's no such thing as The Dorak's Whiskey. I made it up."

Murdoch leaned back in her chair with her legs stretched out in front of her. "Yeah, I know. What I don't know, is why she's lying?" She sighed. "Maybe because she killed Mirabel. Maybe because she was doing something else, she doesn't want me to know about."

The bell over the front door chimed announcing new customers. Harriet and Tammy stepped into the restaurant.

Sybil stuck her head out of the kitchen and said, "Please, have a seat. I'll be with you in a moment."

Larissa called out. "Come join us." Harriet started toward the table. Tammy hesitated and Larissa looked from Tammy to Murdoch as she said, "We promise not to interrogate you during lunch."

Murdoch looked at Tammy. "She's right. No questioning during lunch." She smiled. "It's bad for the digestion."

Murdoch would have preferred to return to her original seat, across from Larissa but couldn't figure out a way to do so without being obvious.

Harriet and Tammy sat down, with Tammy sitting opposite Larissa and Harriet across from Murdoch.

Harriet looked at the faces around the table. "I know we agreed no questioning but, Tammy and I came here to offer information." She looked at Tammy. "Actually, Tammy came with information. I came to eat."

Tammy licked her lips, cleared her throat and said, "It's just that Mirabel has a website. I don't know if you already know that and I don't know if it has anything to do with her...death."

Murdoch studied Tammy for a moment before saying, "Thank you for the information. Yes, we did discover her website and we're looking into it."

Tammy nodded.

Sybil arrived to take their orders. After that an awkward silence fell until Sybil returned with their orders, then Harriet asked, "Sybil, what can you tell me about Edgar?"

Sybil scanned the faces at the table and then looking at Harriet said, "That all depends on what kind of information you're looking for. Are you asking in relation to Mirabel?"

Smiling, Harriet shook her head. "No, chère. I just love that baritone voice. Is he married? Is he seeing someone?"

Sybil relaxed and chuckled. "No, sweetie, he's not seeing anyone, that I know of. Never been married or as far as I know had a serious relationship. But then I've only been in town for a couple of years." She shrugged. "Best I can tell, Molly takes care of all his needs."

Until that statement Murdoch had been focused on her burger. Wiping her hands on her napkin she looked at Sybil. "What do you mean by that?"

"By what? Oh, you mean his sister taking care of his needs." She shrugged. "She seems to like to take care of him."

Murdoch raised an eyebrow.

Sybil realized what Murdoch was thinking. "No, not sexually, just all the other wifely things. Never has liked any of his girlfriends. I kind of thought that maybe she'd get involved with someone, like Mirabel and… You don't think that girl had anything to do with Mirabel's death, do you?"

Before Murdoch could say anything, Larissa laughed. "Hardly. We just don't want our friend here" indicating Harriet "getting her heart broken, again."

Sybil smiled. "I'll be back to check on you folks in a bit. Enjoy."

Harriet smiled conspiratorially. "You two make a good team."

Larissa took a bite of her sandwich to keep from saying something she might regret.

Tammy seemed lost in thought, ignoring the plate of fries in front of her. Then abruptly she said, "I hadn't thought of it like that before but Sybil's right. Any time Edgar started getting serious about a woman, Molly found a way to chase her off."

Silence fell over the table. The only sound for several minutes was utensils on plates and people chewing.

Finally, Murdoch looked at Tammy and said, "That's some car you're driving. Is it a hybrid?"

Tammy laughed. "No. It's a 24-valve dual overhead cam, with 382 horsepower."

Harriet and Larissa tuned out the conversation about cars and enjoyed their meals. Neither of them had any interest in cars, beyond using them to get from one point to another.

# CHAPTER 24

Molly blew into the reading room of her brother's shop and pushed aside the curtain to the main room. "Edgar, I need…"

A woman who looked about sixty was standing in front of her brother, he was holding her hands and talking softly. He stopped speaking when Molly interrupted.

Shooting her a look that would melt an iceberg, he softened his features again before returning his gaze to the woman before him. "Mrs. Cooper, please, come back to see me this evening and I'll have more information for you." He smiled and released her hands. "It would appear that my sister is in need of my attention. I'm sure you understand that family comes first."

Though her expression showed she was not happy the woman said, "Of course. I'll see you around seven then."

"Perfect." He held the door for her and once she was gone, turned the sign to closed, and locked the door. "What the blazes were you thinking? I told you I had a client this afternoon."

Molly waved away his concern and moved their conversation to the back room. She had no intention of being seen talking to her brother by someone passing by.

"She'll be back and even more eager to hear what you have to say because she had to wait. Right now, I need your help."

Edgar was all attention now. It wasn't often that Molly asked him for help. She was always the one helping. "What do you need?"

"When that nosey detective asks you, I need you to tell her that you found me passed out from drinking yesterday early evening."

Edgar stiffened, knowing what he was about to say would make Molly angry. "She's already been around here asking questions. I told her I didn't know where you were yesterday." He watched her jaw tighten with anger. "You didn't kill Mirabel, so just tell her the truth."

"No! Where I was is nobody's business. Be quiet and let me think." Molly walked around the shop running a finger along the counter tops. After a few moments she looked at Edgar. "When she asks you again, and she will, tell her you were embarrassed about me being drunk and that's why you lied."

"Okay, but you know the police have…"

"They have nothing and will have nothing because there's nothing to have. Just do as you're told, and we'll be fine."

Edgar bowed like a courtier from long ago. "As you wish, my lady."

Molly smiled.

# CHAPTER 25

Tammy and Harriet left The Cauldron before Larissa and Murdoch.

Tammy said, "I'm going back to the manor."

"Okay, chère. If you want, I'll walk back with you."

"No, that's all right." She gave Harriet a knowing smile. "I'm sure there's something you want to do here in town. I'll be fine."

Harriet watched Tammy slip between the buildings so she could take the back road to the manor. Then she started toward Edgar's shop.

Harriet stopped in front of his shop window and examined the display. A couple of books, some crystals, and a poster on an easel. The poster promoted his services; private Tarot readings, seances, and private medium sessions to contact those who have passed.

Hmmm. Nothing about fortune telling. Yet last night when Beth, Sara, and I came out of the Crescent Moon. He tried to tell us that he'd seen death, fear, and pain in Larissa's future. We all shook it off as his idea of marketing. Trying to get us in for our own readings. Then when we found out about Mirabel, Sara and Beth, freaked out a bit, especially Beth.

The longer Harriet stood in front of his shop the more uneasy she became. Her experience with Alan Henry had taught her to listen to her instincts. She remembered back to the early days when he'd seemed too good to be true. She'd ignored her gut feeling, that something wasn't quite right, and it had nearly cost her her life.

Charming smile and lovely voice aside, I don't think getting involved with Mr. Edgar Kerry is a good idea.

She took a deep breath and continued down the sidewalk to the next shop. After an hour of browsing and window-shopping Harriet headed back to the manor.

Once Tammy was out of Harriet's sight, she slipped down to the back door of Edgar's shop. As expected, it was unlocked, she slipped inside, and stood there for a few moments while her eyes adjusted to the dark room.

Edgar noticed the change in the light when the back door opened. He waited for whoever had entered to come out front. But no one came.

"Who's there? Come out here."

Tammy flopped into Edgar's reading chair and said, "I don't think so. You come back here."

Moments later she could see a shadow on the curtain to the front of the shop. She knew Edgar was standing there with his eyes closed so they would be adjusted to the dark room before he entered it.

He stepped past the curtain. "What are you doing here?"

"Is that any way to greet an old friend?"

"Mirabel was your friend and yet you're the one who brought that harbinger of death to Cerridwen."

Tammy sighed. "Larissa has seen much death in her short life. She was the cause of none of it. Leave her alone."

Edgar snorted, flipped the metal folding chair around and straddled it, resting his arms on the chair back. "I know what I saw and what I felt."

"You saw her past. Not her future. She didn't even know that Mirabel existed until we found her body. Leave, her, alone. Stop spreading lies about her."

The bells over the front door rang indicating someone had entered.

Edgar called out, "I'll be with you in a moment, please feel free to look around." He stood up and returned his chair to its original position. "I have a customer to see to. You know the way out."

# CHAPTER 26

When Edgar came from the reading room, he expected a customer. He was annoyed to find Det. Murdoch waiting for him, but he forced a smile and said, "What can I do for you today, detective?"

Tammy was headed for the back door when she heard Edgar's greeting. She stopped and moved closer to the curtain. This was a conversation she wanted to hear.

Holding his gaze Murdoch said, "The last time we spoke you told me you didn't know where your sister was when Mirabel was killed. Is that the truth?"

A nervous smile played at Edgar's mouth. "I'm sorry to say, no." He inhaled sharply. "I'm ashamed to admit I do know where my sister was."

"Oh. And where was that?"

"Drunk as a lord in our apartment." He sighed. "You see our parents were both terrible alcoholics and I'm afraid my sister may be heading down that path. I'm sorry I lied to you before, I just… Well, I just don't want it to become common knowledge that she's…well, you know."

Something about Edgar's attitude made Murdoch feel like they weren't alone. As her eyes moved around the room, her gaze stopped at the curtain to the back room.

Maybe there's someone in that backroom. Can't be sure without going back there but… No, not this time. Probably just some fool he's doing a reading for.

"Mr. Kerry, you do understand that this is a murder investigation and that lying to a law enforcement officer is a crime. I could arrest you right now."

Edgar dropped his gaze to the floor. "I understand detective. I am sorry and it won't happen again."

Tammy was impressed with Edgar's acting ability.

"See that it doesn't." Murdoch left the shop and took a deep breath of the clean air to rid herself of the incense burning in the shop.

When they came out of The Cauldron, Larissa went window shopping while Murdoch questioned Edgar about Molly's alibi.

Larissa was across the street when she saw Murdoch come out of Edgar's and moved to join her.

"Well?"

"He confirmed her alibi. Which of course also gives him an alibi." Murdoch sighed. "Which isn't that big of a deal since I can't think of a motive for him. Molly on the other hand, well two of the most common motives for murder are money and jealousy."

When Tammy heard the door close behind Murdoch she peaked around the curtain.

Edgar watched Murdoch until she and Larissa disappeared from sight. "You can come out now."

Tammy called out, "I'd rather you came back here. Your shop has far too much glass for my comfort."

Edgar headed to the reading room and thought, It seems the women in my life are always the ones in control.

Tammy was again sitting in his chair at the reading table, so he again turned the metal folding chair around, sat down and rested his arms on the chair back.

Neither of them spoke for several seconds. Realizing the Edgar wasn't going to start the conversation, Tammy said, "What's this bullshit about Molly being drunk yesterday?"

"What makes you say it's bullshit?"

Tammy silently stared at Edgar.

He pushed the chair against the table as he leaned forward. "You and I both know she had nothing to do with Mirabel's death. So, what does it matter where she was yesterday?"

"If it wasn't Molly, who was it Edgar?"

"How should I know?" He narrowed his eyes and said, "Maybe you should talk to that friend of yours. That Larissa Carpenter."

Tammy snorted. "I already told you, Larissa didn't even know Mirabel existed until we found her body."

Edgar stood up and flipped his chair back to its original position. "I don't care what you say. I know what I saw when I touched her hand."

Tammy stood up and looking into Edgar's eyes, said, "Stop spreading lies about Larissa. What you got a flash of was probably her past, not her future. She's had a great deal of grief in her life, and she doesn't need you adding to it."

Edgar didn't look convinced.

Stepping around the table Tammy got in his personal space. "You know her name. Google her and you'll see what I mean. Regardless, leave her alone."

# CHAPTER 27

As Murdoch and Larissa were walking back to the manor Murdoch's phone rang. She checked the caller ID before answering. "What have you got for me Santos?"

"Quite a bit actually. I'm at the manor."

"I'll be there in ten." She ended the call.

After the brutality of the summer heat, Larissa was enjoying the cooler weather, especially since she knew it wouldn't last. She took a deep breath of the crisp air and decided that this was the perfect opportunity to ask about Deputy Santos.

"So how long has Santos been with the department?"

Murdoch kicked a small stone in the road and watched it skitter down the dirt road kicking up dust along the way. "Don't know. She transferred over to my region about two weeks ago."

"What happened to Brighton?"

"He's on vacation."

"Hmmm. When's he due back?"

Murdoch laughed. "Why don't you like Santos?"

Larissa sniffed. "Never said I didn't like her."

Murdoch could feel the electricity in the air. A breeze carried the vanilla and lemon scent that Larissa wore to Murdoch's nose. She swallowed audibly.

"Yeah, right." She paused. "To answer your unasked question, Santos is an additional deputy. Since crime on the east side of the county seems to be increasing the Sheriff decided to increase staff on this side of the county."

Larissa glanced at Murdoch walking next to her. I wonder what she'd do if I kissed her. Would she be interested? Would she be offended? One of these days I'm going to get up the courage to find out.

"Too bad. I mean, too bad that crime is increasing to that degree."

"Yeah."

When they arrived at the manor neither of them spoke, Larissa headed upstairs, and Murdoch turned left into the living room.

Once on the second floor, Larissa moved to the opposite end of the hall from her room and around the corner. She'd explored earlier and found that there was a study on the second floor that was directly above the first floor living room.

Since the two rooms shared a chimney Larissa figured she might be able to hear Murdoch and Santos' conversation.

"First, a book on the history of Cerridwen. There's not a lot of information of a factual manner, beyond the specifics of who founded the town and when it was founded. The rest of it's about the mediums, spiritualism, covens, pagan rituals, and such."

"What else?"

"Background checks on everyone you listed and a couple of extras."

Murdoch looked up from the book she was skimming. "Oh?" She took the folder Santos offered.

"Yeah, I went ahead and did background on Ms. Colton's business partner. By the way, her last name is also Colton. Stephanie Nicole Colton. Neither of them has ever been married, and the birth certificates of their daughters list the father as unknown."

"We're not the morality police, Santos."

"Well aware of that detective; however, I was curious. So, I did a bit of genealogy on them. The last time one of their female ancestors was married was in 1945. Mary Alicia Hollis married Daniel Colton in 1967. Daniel Colton died before the birth of their daughter Rhonda Daniella. Alicia Marie Hollis married Paul Colton in 1967. He also died in 1967 before the birth of their daughter, Rebecca Pauline Colton in 1967. Daniel and Paul were brothers. After that each subsequent daughter's birth certificate shows father unknown. Rhonda gave birth to Ashely Amanda in 1986 and Rebecca gave birth to Stephanie Nicole in 1986. Amanda and Stephanie gave birth to Cassandra Marie and Priscilla Minerva, respectively, in 2005. Fathers' unknown."

Murdoch processed the information and then with a mischievous smile said, "What would you expect from a bunch of witches?"

Murdoch burst out laughing at the expression on Santos' face. "Whether you and I believe them to be witches or not, is irrelevant. That's how they see themselves and their rituals and beliefs are no stranger than the rituals and beliefs of more accepted religions and philosophies."

Murdoch's laughter brought a smile to Larissa's face, which widened as she imagined the horrified expression on Santos' face at Murdoch's comparison of pagan rituals and those performed by Christian religions.

Santos opened her mouth to speak but Murdoch cut her off. "This isn't a topic that's relevant to the investigation, and I have no intention of getting into a religious or philosophical discussion with you."

The chimney was a wonderful sound conduit, Larissa could hear Murdoch flipping through papers.

"Any criminal record on anyone?"

"No. There have been fraud allegations against almost every person in Cerridwen. Never enough evidence to bother with charges. Let alone get a conviction."

There was silence for several heartbeats and Larissa began to wonder if Murdoch and the deputy had left when Murdoch said, "Tomorrow is a historical tour of the town. I want you and Brighton to take the tour in civvies. Play tourist. I'll text him and let him know what's up."

Murdoch could tell by her expression this wasn't an assignment the deputy was looking forward to.

"Yes, ma'am. Anything else?"

"What about Mirabel Fleur's background? Anything of interest?"

"Not really. She inherited the cottage. It was hers free and clear. Her website and the sale of her organic produce and fresh herbs to some local restaurants provided her with a living income. She recently sold her car, though she still has a valid driver's license. No criminal record. Haven't been able to determine if she has a will or not."

"Head back to the station and keep digging into her background. Check the lawyer that handled her inheritance of the cottage. Maybe she decided to use him for her will." Murdoch moved toward the door. "Oh yeah and dig deeper into Molly and Edgar Kerry. One of them lied to me about where Molly was when Mirabel Fleur was murdered."

"Yes ma'am. Anything else?"

"No. I'll see you tomorrow. You and Brighton come here after the tour."

# CHAPTER 28

Murdoch stood in the doorway of the manor and watched Deputy Santos drive away. She sensed the presence of someone behind her and turned around.

Amanda's face was serene and free of any emotion. "I imagine it's time for you to question me, detective."

Not saying a word Murdoch indicated that they should go to the living room for their talk.

Larissa was standing at the top of the stairs when she saw Murdoch and Amanda enter the living room. She quickly moved back to the upstairs study realizing that Murdoch must be getting ready to interview Amanda.

This would be so much easier if Murdoch would just let me participate in these interviews.

Murdoch sat down in a chair opposite Amanda, making a mental note that Amanda's body language was very open. Both feet flat on the floor and her arms resting on the chair arms.

Placing her phone on the table between them Murdoch went through the ritual of asking permission to record the interview. Amanda agreed.

"What can you tell me about Mirabel Fleur?"

"Mirabel was a valued member of the Cerridwen Coven." Amanda watched Murdoch for a reaction to her inference that Mirabel was a witch.

No reaction, pro or con. Speaks well for the detective.

"Did she have any enemies?"

"None that I know of."

"Do you have any idea who might want to harm her?"

"No."

"Current lovers? Past lovers? Anyone who felt she was a threat to them?"

Amanda smiled. "Mirabel was single at the time of her passing. I'm sure you already know that Tammy Lopez is a past lover. Though I seriously doubt that Tammy had any reason to kill Mirabel. They had remained friends and Mirabel was talking about them getting back together."

"Do you know if Mirabel has a will?"

"Yes. I believe that she used an attorney in Coventry Beach. If I remember correctly, his name is Davis."

"Thank you."

Murdoch leaned back in her chair, watching Amanda's physical reactions to each question.

"Tell me about Molly Kerry."

"Molly. Molly would be the last person to hurt Mirabel. She was in love with her."

"People kill people they love everyday. How did Mirabel respond to Molly's attraction?"

"I suppose they do." Amanda tilted her head a fraction. "Mirabel was kind to the girl, but she had no interest in her as a lover." She paused. "It wasn't just the age difference. Molly being several years younger. And as I said she was thinking

of moving to the city and getting back together with Tammy."
She sniffled. "Actually, this weekend was when she planned
on surprising Tammy. She was going to spend the weekend
and maybe a few more days to try out living in the city before
deciding on a permanent move."

Cassandra stepped into the room. "Mom, the linen delivery
has arrived. He needs your signature."

Murdoch reached for the phone, ending the recording.
"Thank you, Amanda. I may have more questions later."

Amanda stood and inclined her head in acknowledgement.
"Of course, detective. There is a vacant room that you could
stay in if you wish. I'm certain Ms. Carpenter won't object. She
reserved the entire second floor until Tuesday."

Larissa felt a wave of heat wash through her and a tingling
in her extremities at the idea of Murdoch spending the night
just down the hall from her.

"Thank you. I'll keep that in mind."

Murdoch watched Amanda and Cassandra leave. Her mind
went to the information Santos had given her earlier. Wonder
if they're like the black widow spider who kills the male after
mating.

# CHAPTER 29

On her return to Ravenswood Harriet headed for the kitchen. Here she could relax. This was her environment, even if there was nothing for her to do. This was a place where she felt at home.

She located a tea kettle, filled it with water, and set it on the stove to heat. Finding the teas and cups was easy. Amanda kept them on a tray on the counter. There were loose leaf teas to be used with a basket and bag teas for those not interested in the more complex level of tea making. She found a vanilla Lady Grey in the loose-leaf collection and decided that it would be something interesting to try.

Amanda stood in the kitchen doorway, silently watching Harriet.

Without turning around Harriet asked, "Would you like a cup of tea, Amanda?"

"That would be nice. How did you know it was me?"

Harriet shrugged. "Just a feeling. The vanilla Lady grey?"

"Yes, that would be delightful."

Amanda sat at the small table near the window, while she waited for Harriet and her tea. Just as the kettle whistled Amanda reached into a nearby cabinet and pulled out a cookie jar and set it on the table.

"These will go very well with our tea."

When she removed the lid the aroma of lemon and butter wafted from the ceramic container. Amanda placed three thin wafer like cookies on her saucer. Then she tilted the open container toward Harriet, who was seated across from her.

Harriet raised an eyebrow and then placed three of the cookies on her own saucer.

Amanda watched Harriet as she took a bite of a cookie. With her eyes closed Harriet let the small piece of baked heaven dissolve on her tongue.

"Hmmm. Reminds me of the taste of a Madeleine with a different texture."

"Thank you. That's exactly what I was going for." Amanda sipped her tea. "It's my own recipe."

"It's wonderful."

The two women sat in companionable silence for several moments. Then Harriet asked, "What can you tell me about Edgar Kerry?" Before Amanda could object to being questioned. "It has nothing to do with Mirabel's death." She shrugged. "I'm curious for myself. I find him attractive."

Amanda leaned back in her chair and studied Harriet for a moment. "Edgar has a true gift. Let him hold your hands and he can tell you many things about your past and your future. Things you may not want to know." She studied her teacup, running a finger around the rim. "It's the reason he rarely touches people. Sometimes, actually more often than not, he doesn't like what he sees."

Harriet waited for her to continue.

"As for his personal life…" She took a deep breath and moved closer to the table and leaned in. "He was married once. She died in a car accident." Amanda held Harriet's gaze. "It was a one car accident. She lost control and ran into a tree. The car's airbag didn't deploy. Experts examined the vehicle and couldn't find a reason the airbag failed."

She sat back in her chair. "I don't know what the official police report said, if you want to know about that, I suppose you could ask Det. Murdoch."

"I'm not interested in the official report. I'm interested in what you think happened." Harriet could tell that Amanda was hesitant to tell her more. She took a deep breath. "Let me tell you about a recent relationship experience I had. Perhaps then you'll understand my concerns."

Harriet told the story of her engagement to Alan Henry, her breaking off the engagement and the subsequent stalking that ended in Mr. Henry's death at the hands of an FBI agent.

"Do yourself a favor and forget about Edgar Kerry. It's not that I think Edgar had anything to do with his wife's death. However, Molly…well" Amanda sighed.

"I heard that Molly was part of your coven." Larissa isn't the only one who can eavesdrop.

Amanda laughed. "No. She's tried multiple times and I know she's told some people that she's been accepted but she hasn't. Mirabel was teaching her about plants and herbs but she's just not a good fit for our coven." She smiled. "You, on the other hand…"

"Thank you for the honor of your good opinion; however, I have a business to run on the other side of the county." She smiled. "I'm afraid I'll have to remain a solitary."

"I understand but should you ever change your mind, let me know." She paused. "For that matter, if you ever just need to talk, you have family here."

# CHAPTER 30

Tammy was in the garden meditating when her phone rang. She didn't recognize the number and started to send the call to voicemail, then changed her mind.

"Hello."

A male voice with a soft southern accent said, "Hello, have I reached Ms. Tamara Lopez?"

"You have." No one but her mother and other authority figures called her Tamara.

"I am Earl James Davis. I was Ms. Mirabel Fleur's attorney. My condolences on your loss, Ms. Lopez. I'm coming to Ravenswood Manor this evening to read Mirabel's will. Will you be there?"

"Yes. Can you tell me if I'm mentioned in the will?" Without giving him a chance to answer, she continued, "Stupid question. Of course, I am otherwise I wouldn't need to be present."

"I look forward to meeting you, Ms. Lopez."

"Yeah, me too."

\* \* \*

Murdoch was sitting in the living room of Ravenswood Manor when Santos called.

"What have you got, Santos?"

"Attorney Earl James Davis has Ms. Fleur's will."

"Excellent. Who're the beneficiaries?"

"Well, I didn't get to talk to him. He's been in court all day. However, his receptionist told me that he'll be at Ravenswood Manor tonight to read the will to the beneficiaries."

"Okay. That works. Just an FYI, I'll be spending the night at Ravenswood Manor."

Upstairs in the study, Larissa heard this announcement and for a split second her breathing stopped.

She'll be just down the hall tonight. Easy to access. A few steps, a knock on her door and… What? What will I do? Tell her how I feel. Christ, if she hasn't already figured that out, she's not much of a detective, and I know she's a good detective. So, what's stopping her from saying something? Maybe I'm all wrong and she doesn't have any feelings for me.

Larissa left the study and wandered into the garden, looking for a quiet place and some privacy to think through the conundrum that was Det. Angela Murdoch.

# CHAPTER 31

In the early evening Larissa had pizzas delivered to the manor. It made for a very informal meal that people could grab and go or ignore completely. No one really felt like going anywhere so it was perfect and appreciated by all.

For the reading of the will, Amanda made a small buffet of tea, coffee, and cookies for the living room where Earl James Davis would hold court. He'd asked her to make sure that herself and Cassandra were present.

Murdoch stood by the window, watching the others in the room.

Harriet sat in a back corner of the room quietly pretending to read a book. Larissa had asked her to be an observer. She told Harriet, "Unless this was just a random murder, it is most likely that Mirabel's murderer will be at the reading of the will. And an extra pair of eyes is always helpful."

Amanda and Cassandra were in a constant state of movement, either seeing to the buffet or speaking with one of the others. They never stayed with any one person long, before moving to another.

Molly looked like she was trying to find a place to hide. Though when Cassandra approached her, she almost smiled.

Tammy and Larissa were already seated, waiting for the main event. Murdoch watched Larissa whisper something to Tammy. Then Larissa got up and headed to the buffet, where she fixed a small plate and a cup of tea, which she delivered to Tammy.

Murdoch sipped her coffee and tried not to look obvious as she watched Larissa return to the buffet. A noise outside drew her attention.

An F-150 pickup truck pulled onto the grounds. It wasn't new, and it wasn't an antique. It was a work truck that looked as if it was maintained in good working order.

Mr. Davis climbed out of the cab. He was dressed in casual slacks and a polo shirt.

Murdoch watched him stop and study the building for a moment before walking to the entrance. Once he stepped out of sight, Murdoch returned her attention to those in the room. The only thing that had changed was that she didn't see Amanda in the room.

At the open doorway to the room Amanda appeared, with Mr. Davis. "Ladies, if you would all take your seats, we'll get this started." She glanced at Mr. Davis. "I'm sure Mr. Davis has other things to attend to."

Mr. Davis smiled. "Take your time ladies. I don't want to rush anyone. I'm going to get a cup of coffee before I begin." He looked at Amanda standing next to him. "You make the best coffee."

Six chairs formed a semi-circle around a seventh chair facing them. There was a coffee table in the center. Mr. Davis placed his briefcase on the seventh chair and moved to the small buffet Amanda had set up.

Larissa was pouring herself a cup of tea when he stepped up next to her. "Good evening, Ms. Carpenter. It's nice to see you again."

"Mr. Davis, you do get around."

He smiled and said, "What connection do you have to Mirabel?"

"I'm a friend of Tammy Lopez. I'm here for moral support."

He looked around the room, saw Murdoch and looked back to Larissa. "You're sure it's Tammy that you're here for."

Before Larissa could reply Murdoch stepped up. "I take it that you're Mr. Davis. I'm…"

"Yes, I am, and you are Det. Murdoch. I've heard a great deal about you." Murdoch looked at Larissa. "No, not from Ms. Carpenter. From the local news."

"Oh. Yeah. Well, are all the beneficiaries here?"

Mr. Davis looked around the room. "Yes. Everyone is present."

"Excellent." At least, there aren't any surprise beneficiaries. Now the bequests may hold some surprises.

Davis poured a cup of coffee. "Shall we get started?"

He placed the cup on the coffee table, opened his briefcase, pulled out a folder, closed the briefcase, and put it on the floor. When he sat down, he used his foot to push the briefcase under his chair.

Starting at his left he looked at each of the faces in front of him. Larissa was on the end next to Tammy, beside Tammy was Molly, then Cassandra and her mother, Amanda. The empty chair at the other end was meant for Murdoch but she chose to stand.

143

From Murdoch's vantage point she could see the faces of all the beneficiaries. It was the perfect place from which to watch their reactions to the bequests.

"First of all, I've already filed Mirabel's will with the probate court. If you need any explanations of the bequests in the will, I'll be happy to explain them to you, privately." He took a sip of his coffee. "Mirabel named me her Executor. That simply means that I am to carry out her wishes as put forth in her will. All of those present here, with the exception of Det. Murdoch and Ms. Carpenter, are named as beneficiaries in the will." He cleared his throat. "Part of the will states that all beneficiaries be brought together and that I read the bequests to the group."

Larissa wondered if Mr. Davis hadn't noticed Harriet in the corner behind him or if he simply chose to ignore her presence.

He opened the folder on his lap. "I think we can skip over the preamble about sound mind and body and cut right to the chase. First, to Ashley Amanda Colton, I give a copy of my personal recipe book and the pendant she has long admired." Smiling he looked at Amanda. "When the police say we can go into the cottage you can pick up the items. I have here a picture of the pendant in question." He handed Amanda an eight by ten glossy of a pentagram with a dragon wrapped around it.

Amanda glanced at the image and then held it close to her chest. Tears filled her eyes.

Murdoch watched the reactions of the others to what was left to Amanda. No one seemed to take exception to what she received, and she looked pleased.

"To Cassandra Marie Colton, I leave a selection of herbs and other plants" Davis looked up from the document "Cassandra, there's a long list here of the plants. When we're finished here, I'll give you a copy of the will." He paused. "Actually, all beneficiaries will get a copy of the will before I leave tonight. Mirabel also left you a set of cat earrings that you admired." He handed her an eight by ten of the cat earrings.

Cassandra accepted the picture without looking at it. Her face remained passive, unreadable. She showed neither joy nor disappointment at her bequest.

Murdoch thought Cassandra's body language was tight. She's suppressing some kind of emotion and I don't think it's joy. I think she's royally pissed. Wonder what she expected to get?

Mr. Davis took a sip of his coffee and continued. "To Molly Kerry, I leave a selection of plants, and a half-acre of land, so that you may start your own garden. Once the probate is complete, I'll provide you with the deed for the land."

Murdoch felt that Molly was conflicted about her gift from Mirabel.

Before anyone could ask a question Mr. Davis said, "All my remaining worldly goods and possessions, I leave to Tamara Jane Lopez, with the proviso that she live in the cottage and run the herb and produce business. Should she decide that she doesn't want to occupy the cottage and run the business, then all my remaining worldly goods and possessions will go to Molly Kerry, with the exception of the ring that Tamara gave me two years ago."

Mr. Davis looked at the group before him, thankful that this wasn't a task many of his clients asked him to perform. He, once again cleared his throat, stood, and pulled his briefcase from under the chair. He placed the briefcase on the chair, opened it and removed four copies of the will.

Placing the stack of documents on the coffee table he said, "Ladies, thank you for your attention." He pointed at the four folders on the table. "I've included a business card in each folder. If you should have any questions, please, feel free to call me."

Then he stepped over to Tammy. "Ms. Lopez, here's the key to the cottage. As soon as the police release it, I'm sure they'll give your whatever keys are currently in their possession." His gaze took in all the women before him. "Again, I'm sorry for your loss."

Tammy wrapped her hand tightly around the key. "Thank you, Mr. Davis."

Davis turned to Amanda. "Thank you for your hospitality, Amanda. Hopefully, the next time we meet it will be under more pleasant circumstances."

"One can hope. I'll see you out."

Amanda and Davis started to leave. At the doorway he stopped, turned into the room, and said, "There's a message in the will for each of you. I suggest you read it and take it to heart." He turned and left the room, with Amanda.

Murdoch continued to watch everyone. He saw Larissa lean in and whisper something in Tammy's ear. Looks like whatever she said confused Tammy.

Molly stepped in front of Tammy, who was still seated and demanded, "Are you keeping the cottage?"

146

Tammy stood up forcing Molly to take a step back. Larissa rose with Tammy a hand on Tammy's arm. Tammy's expression had changed from one of confusion to one of anger.

Larissa looked at Molly and said, "I don't think now is the time for this discussion. Everyone's emotions are a bit too raw."

Molly looked from Tammy to Larissa. "Who do you think you are? Stay out of this."

Larissa gently but firmly moved Tammy aside and standing in front of Molly replied, "I'm her friend."

Molly scoffed. "Friend, huh. Well, friend watch out for that one she'll desert you when you need her most. She's a heartbreaker. If Mirabel wasn't dead, you could ask her." Without another word she turned and stormed from the house.

Seconds later Tammy bolted for the stairs. Larissa started to go after her, but Murdoch said, "Let her go. She probably needs some time alone."

"Yes, I suppose so." Larissa picked up one of the folders that held the will. "I'll make sure she gets this."

Murdoch nodded and crooked a finger at Harriet. Harriet rose to join her and Larissa, as she approached, Murdoch said, "Walk with me, ladies."

In the garden, Murdoch walked all the way to the back gate before speaking. She looked at the two women with her and said, "I want you two to be extra careful. While Molly may be under suspicion, I'm still not sure she's the one." She glanced across the garden at the house. "It could still be someone else." She paused. "I'll be in the room between Tammy and Harriet tonight."

Harriet smiled. "I feel safer already."

Larissa kept how Murdoch's proximity made her feel, to herself.

# CHAPTER 32

When Tammy opened her door to the balcony, Murdoch turned her lights out. Looking around the curtains from a dark room into the dark night let her see without being seen. Tammy never appeared on the balcony, so Murdoch figured she just wanted some fresh air.

Before Murdoch turned her lights back on, she heard another door open, and decided to leave her lights off.

Too far away to be Harriet's door, so it must be Larissa.

Larissa stepped onto the balcony and looked out over the garden. It seemed amazing that less than twenty-four hours ago she had followed Tammy to a dead body. She looked over her shoulder and noticed that further down the balcony, Tammy's door was open.

For a moment she stared at the rectangle of light spilling out of Tammy's room, as if it led to an unknown universe.

As she walked past Harriet's room, Larissa noticed light around the closed curtains.

So, Harriet's still awake.

There was no light around Murdoch's curtains.

Either she's asleep or sitting in the dark.

Hearing footsteps on the balcony, Murdoch returned to the window.

Larissa. Headed to Tammy's room.

Murdoch heard Larissa say, "We need to talk." However, she was unable to hear Tammy's reply.

Tammy half-smiled. "Those words are never a good sign. Come on in." She was sitting on the edge of the bed, staring into a glass of bourbon. She looked up at Larissa. "Can I get you something?"

Quietly, Murdoch opened her own door a crack, hoping it would allow her to hear the conversation next door, but she still couldn't make out what Tammy was saying.

Murdoch's desire to hear both sides of the conversation outweighed her caution. She opened her door and stepped onto the balcony. Keeping her eyes on the garden, she stood at the railing, and took a deep breath, hoping that no one would notice her.

Here she could hear both women.

"No thanks. I'm fine."

Tammy sighed. "What is it you want to talk about?" She rolled the glass between her hands, occasionally looking at it as if she wasn't sure what it was.

Larissa sighed and sat down in the chair near the window. "I'm not really sure where to begin."

Tammy looked up and saw Murdoch standing at the balcony railing, took a deep breath and said, "How about if I help you out. You want to stay friends, but the benefits have been cancelled." She downed the contents of the glass, took the bottle from the nightstand, and splashed some into the glass.

Larissa nodded her head. "Yeah, I suppose that's as good a way as any to put it." She tilted her head and smiling asked, "How did you know?"

Tammy laughed. "Are you kidding? A blind man could see how you feel about a certain detective."

Larissa chuckled. "Then why can't the detective see it?"

"Maybe she does but..." Tammy fell silent.

"But what?"

"Perhaps it's all that money you've got. It can be a bit, intimidating. You know." She paused, took a sip of her bourbon, and said, "Maybe you need to make the first move." She shrugged. "What's the worst that can happen?"

Larissa had tilted the chair back on its two back legs. "Hmm. The worst that could happen would be that I find out she doesn't feel the same way and it damages our friendship." She dropped the chair onto all four legs. "I'm not sure I'm willing to risk that."

Murdoch returned to her room and closed the door. She'd heard all she needed to hear and didn't want to be standing out there when Larissa left Tammy's room.

Larissa stood up and looked out the window. "What do you plan to do with your inheritance?" She moved to lean against the door jamb.

Tammy sat back on the bed. "Well, if I wouldn't live in Cerridwen with Mirabel, I'm sure as hell not living here without her. But I understand why Murdoch wants me to say I'm staying." She burped. "If Mirabel was killed for the cottage, I'm bait."

Larissa walked to the bed, took the glass from Tammy's hand, and picked up the bottle. She walked to the dresser and set them down. "Being bait, is bad enough. Being drunk bait, is unacceptable." She headed out the door, stopped in the doorway, smiled at Tammy, and said, "Get some sleep."

Tammy rolled onto her side placing her back to the door.

Larissa considered closing Tammy's door but decided against it. The fresh air will do her good and she's got Murdoch next door and Harriet and I are just a couple of doors away.

Standing outside Tammy's room, Larissa was torn between returning to her room and going to Murdoch's.

I'll check it as I walk by and if it's still dark, I'll keep going. If the lights are on, I'll knock.

Even with the curtains closed she could tell the room was dark.

With a heavy sigh Larissa stepped next door to Harriet's and knocked.

"Come on in, chère."

Larissa entered the room. Harriet took one look at her and shook her head. "Girl, you need to deal with this thing between you and Murdoch."

Flopping into the nearest chair, Larissa said, "Yes, I know."

"So?"

"So, I don't know how I want to deal with it."

"Hmmm. I take it you've ended things with Tammy."

"Yeah." She shrugged. "We'll still be friends but…"

"Hmmm. What about Murdoch?" Like Tammy, Harriet had seen Murdoch on the balcony a bit earlier. "When did you talk to Tammy?"

"Just before I came here."

"Uh huh. Exactly what did you two talk about?"

Larissa sat up in her chair and leaned forward with her elbows on her knees. "Why?"

"Well, Murdoch was out on the balcony just a bit ago. It's possible that she overheard your conversation with Tammy."

"Seriously?" Larissa hung her head. "Shit! Tell me you're joking."

Harriet shook her head. "I wouldn't kid you about a thing like that."

"Maybe it's best that she heard. Go talk to her. You can't keep ignoring the big red elephant in the room."

"Red? Most people say the big white elephant in the room. Why red?"

Harriet smiled. "Because chère, red is the color for passion."

Larissa laughed, stood, and stretched. "This weekend has been one huge dumpster fire. I think next time I want to give friends a quiet weekend away, I'll just pay for everybody to go to different locations instead of a group event. Maybe that way at least odds are someone will have a great weekend."

Harriet gave Larissa a big hug. "Talk to her."

"Yeah, I'll think about it. Goodnight, Harriet."

# CHAPTER 33

Back in her room Larissa paced and argued with herself about the best course of action to take.

What the hell is wrong with me? She's just a woman. I've made decisions on dealing with millions of dollars in less time than this.

Pacing the room her eyes spotted Tammy's copy of the will laying on the dresser.

I wonder what that note Mirabel left for everyone says. I'm not mentioned in the will. Still, I'm sure that if I asked Tammy what the note said, she'd tell me.

Larissa rested her hand on the document for a moment as she debated with herself about reading its contents. She quickly scanned the bequests and then at the end she found the note that the attorney had mentioned.

"Know that each of you hold a special place in my heart. Though I am no longer with you in the physical world, know that I will always be alive in your thoughts. As long as there is one alive who remembers me, I live. Don't waste your life mourning my passing, rather rejoice in the time we shared. Think of the fun we had and smile. May you be happy as long as you live and may you live as long as you're happy.

So mote it be."

She read the message multiple times, letting the words sink in. Then she closed the folder and returned it to the top of the dresser. For several heartbeats she left her hand resting on the folder, the way one would rest their hand on a bible.

She closed her eyes and took more than a few deep breaths. Opened her eyes, picked up her phone and wrote a text to Murdoch.

We need to talk. Are you awake? If so, no need to reply. Just come to my room.

For several seconds, her finger hovered over the send command, then she pressed it and waited.

Murdoch's phone chimed. From the notification sound she knew it was a text from Larissa. She read the text message.

Grabbing her travel mug of cold coffee Murdoch started out the door. Then she stopped and smiling, texted Larissa.

On my way.

As she stepped out onto the balcony, she could see Larissa's door was open. In the open doorway, she paused.

Larissa was sitting in a chair to the right of the doorway. To the left of the doorway was another chair.

"Please, come in and have a seat."

Murdoch settled into the chair, placed her travel cup on the floor, and rested her arms on the chair arms. She mirrored Larissa's body language. With both feet flat on the floor, her body language gave every indication that she was open, with nothing to hide.

Larissa started at Murdoch's feet and slowly brought her eyes up to meet the detectives. As they held each other's gaze, Larissa asked, "Did you overhear my conversation with Tammy earlier tonight?"

"Technically it was last night. It is after midnight."

"Evasive response. Not a lie but not a yes or no answer." Larissa drew in a deep breath. "Let me rephrase the question. Did you overhear the conversation I had with Tammy Lopez at approximately 10:30 p.m. last night?"

"Yes." Murdoch's voice was barely audible. She cleared her throat and in a more audible voice said, "Yes."

Unable to sit still Larissa stood and asked, "What do you have to say about what you heard?"

Murdoch got to her feet and stepped into Larissa's space. Her arms hung at her sides. She inhaled Larissa's intoxicating scent as she brought her lips closer to Larissa's.

Larissa looked into Murdoch's eyes, searching for the answer to her question.

Before Murdoch could answer, the sound of someone pounding up the stairs drew their attention to the hallway.

"Murdoch! Murdoch! She's gone. Cassandra's missing."

# CHAPTER 34

Murdoch and Larissa raced to the hallway. Amanda was already at Murdoch's room door pounding on it.

"Amanda!"

The frantic woman stopped with her fist halfway to the door, turned and saw Murdoch standing next to Larissa. Realizing she may have interrupted something she began, "I'm sorry. It's just…"

"Don't apologize. Your child is missing." Larissa brought Amanda into her room. "Here sit down." She placed Amanda on the bench at the end of the bed.

Murdoch squatted down in front of Amanda. By the time Larissa had poured Amanda a shot of bourbon, Harriet was standing in the doorway.

"What's happened, chère?"

Larissa handed Amanda the glass and turned to Harriet. "Cassandra is missing."

Harriet moved into the room and sat next to Amanda.

Murdoch said, "I take it it's not normal behavior for her to sneak out at night."

"No! She knows that whether I approve or not, I won't stop her from going to parties and such. At least that way I know where she is and most of who she's with."

"Okay. Can you think of anyone she might sneak off to see?" Murdoch looked from the distraught mother to Larissa and Harriet, then she stood up.

Realizing Tammy was the only person not present she asked, "Where's Tammy?"

Larissa stepped onto the balcony and tried the door to Tammy's room. It opened on an empty room. She hit the light switch by the door. Tammy's phone was on the dresser and next to it was the key to the cottage.

Larissa grabbed the phone and the key before returning to her room.

Murdoch met her on the balcony outside Harriet's room. "Tammy's gone, too."

While she waited for Santos to answer, Murdoch asked Larissa, "Did she pack up and go or just go?"

Larissa held up Tammy's phone. "I can tell you she didn't take her phone."

"Hello." Santos' voice was groggy.

"Santos, wake up." She paused but not long enough for Santos to say anything. "We have two missing people. Tammy Lopez and Cassandra Colton. Wake up Brighton and both of you get to Ravenswood Manor. Now." Murdoch ended the call.

Murdoch turned to head back to Larissa's room. Larissa put a hand on her arm and whispered, "Read this text Tammy got." She handed Murdoch Tammy's phone.

"Meet me at the cottage if you want to know who killed Mirabel." It was from an unknown number.

Murdoch checked the time. The text had come in fifteen minutes ago. Doing some quick calculations in her head

Murdoch decided that Tammy should be halfway to the cottage as they were speaking. "Look, she has to be on foot. One of us would have heard that car of hers. I think we still need to search this house before we go tearing off to the cottage."

Larissa didn't agree but this wasn't the time to argue. She figured that searching the house would take less time than the argument. Murdoch put Tammy's phone in her pocket and she and Larissa returned to Larissa's room.

"Harriet, stay here with Amanda. Larissa's going to help me search the building and the grounds." She looked at Larissa. "Check all the rooms on this floor and the attic. I'm heading downstairs. Meet me in the kitchen when you're done."

Larissa raced down the hallway throwing open room doors. In each room she opened the bathroom doors, looked behind shower curtains, and searched closets. The only rooms she didn't search were Nicole and Stephanie's suite. Those doors were locked.

She pulled the stairs down that led to the attic. Using her flashlight, she gave the room a quick but thorough search.

Nothing!

As she was watching the attic stairs disappear into the ceiling, she realized the one place she hadn't looked – under the beds. As she moved back down the hallway she checked under every bed.

Larissa paused in her doorway long enough to meet Harriet's gaze and shake her head before heading downstairs. She met Murdoch at the foot of the stairs. They both looked into the kitchen, the pantry was open and there was no place else in that room for someone to hide.

Murdoch indicated Larissa should follow her as she moved down the hallway to the back door. Standing in the doorway Murdoch moved into the yard to the right and motioned Larissa to check to the left.

It didn't take them long to do a search of the garden and the shed on the north side of the house. Murdoch climbed the north side stairs to the balcony and Larissa came up from the south.

Back in Larissa's room Murdoch said, "They must have gone out the front door." She looked at Larissa. "One of us would have heard the gate squeak if they went out the back."

"The security lights didn't come on and the gate doesn't squeak anymore. Someone oiled it." Larissa muttered.

"What?"

"Just now when we were out back, the security lights didn't come on."

"What security lights?"

Amanda said, "At the bottom of the stairs from here, there are security lights. They're for safety in case a guest is coming or going late at night." She stood up. "They were working earlier this evening. I always check them before I go to bed."

"Amanda what's the fastest way to Mirabel's cottage?"

"Follow the road that leads to the parking lot, just before it reconnects with Ravens Way there'll be a road to the left. It's called Witch Way, though the signage is poor. It will take you to Mirabel's cottage."

# CHAPTER 35

I beat Murdoch out the door and headed for my Prius. While I'm sure Murdoch would have preferred to drive, she didn't waste time arguing about it. Instead, she climbed into the passenger seat.

Since the roads were deserted, I ignored any pretense at obeying speed limits. Even without seeing the sign for Witch Way, I spotted the road, slowed enough to make the turn safely and then hit the gas again.

I knew it couldn't be very far to Mirabel's cottage. After rounding a sharp turn in the road, I kept glancing to my left. I could see that there were lights on in the cottage, allowing me to catch glimpses of it through the trees.

As we approached the driveway, I turned off the headlights and slowed enough that the electric engine took over.

Murdoch smiled. "Smooth. I forget how quiet this thing can be."

"Thanks for not arguing about which vehicle to take. How do you want to handle this?"

"Hmmm. Since I'm not sure what this is, I don't know." Murdoch studied the cottage for a second. "You didn't happen to grab the key to the cottage when you were in Tammy's room did you?"

I smiled and held up the solitary key. Murdoch held out her hand and I dropped the key into it.

"I want you to go around to the kitchen door. Come at it as if you came from the woods. I'll come in the front door." Murdoch sighed heavily. "From there we'll just have to wing it."

Staying close to the woods I skirted the edge of the yard until I reached the path to the woods. Then I moved through the yard toward the house.

I couldn't see Cassandra; however, I could see Tammy. She was standing facing the island, sinks behind her. If it was Cassandra she was talking to, then she had her back to the door.

I figured Cassandra had to be close to the island or I'd be able to see her through the open doorway.

As I walked toward the kitchen doorway, I took a deep breath and started talking. "Tammy, what the hell are you doing here? You know this is still an active..."

Standing in the doorway I faced Cassandra pointing a gun in my direction and backing away from me.

"Whoa!" Instinctively, I raised my hands. My eyes moved from Cassandra to Tammy and back several times. "What's going on here, Cassandra?"

"Why are you here?" Cassandra's voice was angry. "This is between her and me."

"Your mother woke up and couldn't find you. She was worried." I glanced at Tammy. "She woke everyone up. That's when we realized that Tammy was also missing." I kept my voice low and non-judgmental. "Cassandra, what's going on here?"

An evil grin widened her mouth. She used the gun to motion me toward the island. As I moved to my right I also moved forward. That way it would be harder for her to move me to the other side of the island. The more distance I could keep between Tammy and me the better.

The smell of mint was strong. I looked at the glass in front of Tammy. I knew what it contained, Pennyroyal oil.

"What's going on is this. Tammy here is writing her confession and suicide note, all in one."

"What's she confessing to?"

"She's the reason Mirabel is dead!"

"Wow. I had no idea. You should turn her over to Det. Murdoch."

Cassandra laughed. "I don't think that will work."

"Why not? I mean if she killed Mirabel then the law will deal with her."

"No! She's going to die the same way Mirabel did." She aimed the gun at Tammy. "Drink it or I shoot."

Hesitantly, Tammy started to reach for the shot glass.

"Have you told her what she'll be drinking?"

"Well, duh, it's poison."

"Of course, but don't you think the anticipation of knowing what the poison will do to her should be part of her punishment?"

"I knew I liked you for a reason." A malicious smile spread across Cassandra's face. "It will be a slow painful death. Stomach cramps, nausea, vomiting. Your organs will begin to slowly fail. Depending on how healthy you are will determine how long it will take you to die." She laughed. "And the best part, there is no antidote."

Tammy pulled her hand away from the glass. Her eyes were wide with fear. "You're crazy!"

"That may be but I'm also the one holding the gun. Now drink."

"No!" Tammy took a step backward.

"Well then, how about if instead of shooting you, I shoot her." Cassandra aimed the gun in my direction and stepped closer to me. "At this range I can't miss. One bullet right between the eyes. Her death will be all your fault too. Just like it's your fault that Mirabel is dead."

"You didn't mean to kill Mirabel did you, Cassandra?" I was stalling and hoping that my voice would mask the sound of Murdoch approaching behind her.

"No! It was only supposed to make her sick so she'd stay, and I could take care of her."

"What happened, Cassandra? What went wrong?"

"I heard her and my mother talking, and she was planning on leaving this weekend. I had to hurry. I didn't read all the information. I skimmed the section on Pennyroyal oil. Stomach cramps, vomiting. Just a little discomfort. I figured it was just what I needed, and the plant was right here in the garden."

"How did you create the oil?"

"I'd borrowed Mirabel's steam distiller a while back and…" Cassandra sobbed and for a nano-second she dropped her guard, but it wasn't enough. Just as I was thinking about moving on her, she was back on point.

She narrowed her eyes and looked at me. "Why did you have to come here? Now I'll have to kill you too." Then a thought must have occurred to her. "That's all right. I'll just have her rewrite her suicide confession note to include you."

My eyes were focused on Murdoch who was coming up behind Cassandra. Unfortunately, she was still a good ten feet away and Cassandra was within three feet of me. It was time to bluff. I looked to my left and smiled as if I'd just seen the cavalry arriving.

Cassandra turned her head to look behind her. I grabbed the gun by the barrel with my left hand and used my right elbow to connect with Cassandra's face as I spun around. The gun went off.

Murdoch moved in and caught Cassandra as she went down.

# CHAPTER 36

Murdoch lowered the unconscious Cassandra to the floor. Checking her pulse she said, "She's alive." She stood up. "Did anyone get hit?"

We both looked at Tammy, who was standing with her back to us. It looked like she was staring out the window over the sink.

"Tammy! Tammy!" She finally turned around. Her face was white as a sheet. "Did you get hit?"

Rather than answer she pointed at the bullet hole in the window. I swallowed hard realizing how close the bullet must have come to her head.

Moving to her side of the island I dragged a stool with me. "Here. Sit down." Realizing that a stool wasn't the best seat I moved the thing close enough to the island that Tammy could use the counter for support.

I still had the long-barrel revolver in my left hand. Tammy was looking at it as if it might go off again, so I placed it on the counter and pushed it away from us.

Then I heard Murdoch on the phone. "Brighton. Are you and Santos at the manor? Good. I need medical and forensics. After you call for that, get over here to help with the crime scene. Amanda can tell you the quickest route to take. The blue Prius in the road will let you know you're in the right place." Murdoch ended the call before Brighton could start asking questions.

"They'll be here shortly."

"What the hell is going on here?" Molly was standing in the kitchen's open doorway, taking in the scene before her.

Murdoch was standing near Cassandra who still lay unconscious on the floor. Tammy and I were on the far side of the kitchen island with the gun laying nearby.

Before I knew it, Molly had the gun in her hand. She directed her words to Murdoch. "Which one of them killed Mirabel? Huh? Tell me!"

I watched Murdoch who remained focused on Molly. She knew if she gave any indication as to which person in the room had killed Molly's beloved Mirabel, things could escalate fast.

"Molly, give me the gun." Murdoch stepped toward her. "You don't want to do this. Give me the gun now and we'll forget all about this incident."

She aimed the gun at Tammy. "Was it her?"

"Molly, would Mirabel want you to take the law into your own hands? Huh? I don't think so. Everything I've heard about Mirabel tells me she was a gentle and forgiving soul."

"Stop! One more step and I'll shoot...Larissa."

Murdoch stopped moving and put her hands up. "Okay. Okay. But you have to know I have deputies on the way. As well as an ambulance for Cassandra." She took a slow deep breath. "That revolver is a six shooter. It's down to five bullets. If you shoot the four of us. That leaves you with one bullet.

Think Molly. I know who killed Mirabel. Am I going to tell you? No! At least, not as long as you're holding that gun."

The sound of approaching vehicles could be heard. "Once the others get in here and see you holding a gun on us. I won't be able to keep you from being charged. Give me the gun."

Molly looked around the room, trying to decide what to do. With no time to spare she put the gun back on the kitchen island. As Brighton, Santos, and Amanda came through the front door Murdoch grabbed the gun by the barrel. With her arm hanging down next to her, the gun was out of sight.

Amanda ran to Cassandra and dropped to the floor next to her. Cradling her daughter's head she looked up at Murdoch. "Is my baby going to be all right?"

Murdoch gave Brighton a questioning look.

"Sorry boss. She wouldn't tell us how to get here if we didn't bring her with us."

Murdoch sighed and turned to Amanda. "Most likely, she just got knocked out. The medics should be here soon."

Cassandra began to moan. She opened her eyes and seemed to quickly figure out the situation. "Mom, what happened? Why am I…" she tried to sit up and fell back into her mother's arms.

"Shhh. Be still. Ambulance is on the way. Just stay still." Looking at her daughter's face she brushed the long blonde hair back and noticed the bruise beginning to show on the side of her face.

With angry eyes she brought her gaze up to Murdoch. "Who did this?"

Murdoch moved so that Amanda could see the revolver she was still holding by the barrel.

I was watching her for a reaction and saw the look of recognition on her face when she saw the firearm.

It's her gun."It's a long story and we'll go into it later. This isn't the time or place."

Amanda started to get up, but Cassandra said, "Please, don't leave me Momma."

Amanda sat back down and continued to cradle Cassandra. "I'll never leave you baby."

Seconds later the EMTs came through the front door. Murdoch didn't wait for them to ask what happened, she said, "She was hit on the head pretty hard. Unconscious for three to five minutes."

They took her vitals, checked her pupils, and then loaded her into the ambulance. Amanda went with her.

# CHAPTER 37

"Brighton, bag that glass, carefully. I don't know if that poison can be absorbed through the skin or if it has to be ingested." Murdoch smiled. "So don't get any of it on you."

Brighton adjusted his nitrile gloves and carefully placed the glass in an evidence bag.

"Santos, follow the ambulance. No one but her mother and medical professionals is allowed to talk to Cassandra Colton. Make sure you Mirandize her."

"What's the charge, boss?"

Murdoch held the deputy's gaze. "The murder of Mirabel Fleur and the attempted murder of Tammy Lopez." Santos hesitated, a look of shock on her face.

Murdoch ordered. "Go!"

Santos did a smart about face and was out the door.

Murdoch turned to Molly. "Ms. Kerry, what brought you to the cottage tonight?"

"I, uh, I couldn't sleep. So, I decided to visit Mirabel's garden. It was her favorite place. I wanted to be close to her spirit. I was almost here when I heard the gunshot."

She looked from Murdoch to me to Tammy and then back to Murdoch. "Why? Why would Cassandra kill Mirabel?"

I knew Murdoch wasn't going to answer Molly's question.

I took a deep breath. "She was afraid of losing Mirabel to Tammy and the city. She didn't intend to kill her. She only wanted to make her sick enough that she'd have to stay. Then Cassandra would take care of her."

Molly sniffed the air. "Mint. Mint." Her eyes widened and she looked at me. "Pennyroyal oil?"

Molly sank to the floor sobbing. Murdoch started toward her, but Molly held up a hand to stop her. "No, please, just let me be here for a little while."

Murdoch stepped back. "Sure." Still holding the revolver by its barrel, she said, "Brighton, I need an evidence bag."

Examining the weapon through the clear bag, Brighton said, "Nice one."

Molly stood up from the floor. "Cassandra should have known that Pennyroyal oil is fatal and has no antidote."

Murdoch studied Molly. "She claimed she wasn't aware at the time that it would kill Mirabel. Said she just skimmed the information."

"Bullshit! I don't believe it. That girl knows herbs and poisons better than I do. I find it hard to believe she didn't know that Pennyroyal oil would be fatal."

# CHAPTER 38

As I sat watching Harriet clean up before closing time, my thoughts wandered back to the events at Ravenswood Manor. When I reached the departure of Sara and Beth, I stopped.

"Harriet, do you remember when Sara and Beth left the manor?"

"Sure, chère. What about it?"

I sighed. "I don't know exactly. It just seemed like they, no, not they, but Beth seemed unusually upset. It was as if she couldn't wait to get out of there." For a moment I stared into my teacup as if in the shallow depths of the amber liquid it held were the answers I was looking for. I brought my eyes up to Harriet, standing behind the counter. She was watching me.

"What happened at the Crescent Moon that night?"

Harriet studied me and then took a deep breath. Leaving the cleaning cloth on the counter, she walked over and sat down across from me. I tolerated her staring into my eyes for several seconds before demanding, "What?"

"I'm concerned about you."

My suspicions were aroused. Somehow whatever happened after Tammy, and I left the group in downtown Cerridwen had something to do with me. "Talk to me, Harriet."

"That night after we left the Crescent Moon, we ran into Edgar."

"So?"

She sighed. "So, he told us all about what he'd seen when he touched your hand during his reading."

I searched my mind trying to remember exactly what he'd said to me. "All he told me was about my love life. A woman with a dangerous job and I wasn't sure if she felt about me the way I felt about her." I shrugged. "That's why I thought you'd given him information. I mean, how else could he know those things?"

Harriet laughed. "I went to see him after the reading of the will. I wanted to know what he told you the cards said. Then I questioned him about the stuff he'd said to me and the others when we were leaving the Crescent Moon."

"And?" Harriet didn't speak right away.

I jumped up from the table, knocking over the chair I'd been in. My fists resting on the table I leaned in and said, "Damn it, woman! Sometimes getting you to talk is like trying to get an honest answer from a politician. Tell me what he said."

"Since you ask so nicely, he said that when he touched your hand he saw death, fear, and pain." She paused. "He did admit that he sees past as well as future events when he touches a person."

I did my best to keep my face from showing anything while inside I was screaming.

Harriet narrowed her eyes as she studied me. "Don't be taking his nonsense to heart, chère. Those are three things that follow all of us around." She almost smiled as she continued, "Kind of like getting your heart broken. If you live long enough it's inevitable."

I knew she was right, but it didn't do anything to ease the guilt I felt. It did seem like death followed me around or in the case of Mirabel, preceded me. With Murdoch being in such a dangerous job, was it a good idea for me to pursue her?

Maybe she'd be safer if I weren't around her. Though I didn't even know Mirabel. My only connection to her was Tammy. Maybe that was enough.

My thoughts were interrupted by Harriet. "What are you thinking about?"

"Huh? Oh, I was just wondering why his words had such a strong impact on Beth. Any ideas?"

"Beth is very emotionally fragile. I'm not sure exactly what's going on with that one. I do know that his words and then learning of Mirabel's death were enough to send her running back to Central City."

I picked up the chair I'd knocked over and sat down.

Death, fear, and pain. Harriet was right, they're three elements of the human condition that none of us escape. But...but what? They do seem to spend an inordinate amount of time in my vicinity.

Once again, Harriet's voice pulled me out of my thoughts. "You okay, chère?"

I forced a smile and said, "Of course. Just a lot of hocus pocus nonsense."

Harriet rose and returned to her cleaning behind the counter. It was ten minutes to closing and then Harriet was going home to pick up Cleo and they were coming to my house for dinner.

174

The bell over the door chimed. The breeze that came in through the open door carried her scent mingled with the salty air.

Murdoch.

"Hey chère."

"Hello Harriet." She turned those magnificent grey eyes my way. "Larissa."

"Hello Murdoch."

Harriet smiled. "Let me guess. Coffee, black and one beignet."

"You know me too well, Harriet."

As she walked past me to the counter, her scent was no longer muted by the smell of the sea. Honey and vanilla. Damn that woman always smells good enough to eat.

I sat up straighter in my chair and asked, "How goes the case against Cassandra?"

Half sitting on a stool at the counter, she sighed, "You know I shouldn't be talking about the case."

"Yeah, so?"

Laughing she turned from the counter to face me. "What the hell, you know pretty much everything already. Cassandra claims it was an accident. Molly calls bullshit. The DA is thinking of trying Cassandra as an adult."

"Wow!"

"She'll be seventeen next week." Murdoch sighed. "She'd have probably gotten off with manslaughter and been tried as a teen if she hadn't tried to kill Tammy, too."

"Sadly, I tend to believe Molly on this one. According to what Amanda told Tammy, Mirabel thought Cassandra was a natural with plants. That she understood botany and such the way some people get technology. She had to know her stuff if that was the case." I sipped my tea. "You know I did some research on that Pennyroyal oil. Ten milliliters is a fatal dose. I read the forensics report on the dose she wanted Tammy to drink. It had an ounce of the oil in it. That's three times the fatal dose."

Murdoch tilted her head and studied me. "How did you get access to the forensics report? No, never mind. I don't want to know."

I laughed and said, "Good because I wasn't going to tell you anyway." While Murdoch contemplated what I said, I continued, "Speaking of Molly. Did you ever find out where she really was when Mirabel was killed?"

Murdoch smiled. "Yeah, she was in bed with Sybil. She didn't want her brother or anyone else to find out." She paused. "You know, if I tell the DA about what you said regarding Cassandra's knowledge of poisons and plants, you'll most likely be called to testify to that."

"Hmm. Yeah, I'd really rather not. I know Molly's going to have to testify about Cassandra's herbal knowledge. Maybe her testimony will be enough."

"Yeah, but you're still going to be called to testify about that night at the cottage."

I shrugged. "Unless the DA works out some kind of deal where this doesn't go to trial."

Murdoch looked at me suspiciously. "What do you know?"

"Me? I don't know anything." I shrugged. "I just figure that trying a good-looking young girl like Cassandra could be a publicity nightmare. I mean, I know the DA wants to appear tough on crime, but I don't think a beautiful young teenager with her mother and both in tears will play well in the press."

"Hmm. Have you talked to Tammy lately?"

Sighing I said, "The last time I saw Tammy was when I went with her to the cottage. She turned the property over to Molly. She's leaving the area as soon as the trial is over, which is probably for the best." I paused. "She told me she'd spoken with Amanda. She wanted to know about the whole thing with Mirabel moving to the city. Turns out that Mirabel was planning on coming for the weekend to visit and decide if she was willing to move there."

"In other words, Mirabel hadn't yet decided to move to the city." Murdoch looked at Larissa pointedly. "That's the kind of misunderstanding that happens when people eavesdrop and only get part of the story."

Harriet placed a large to-go cup and a paper bag on the counter next to Murdoch. "Here you go chère."

Murdoch dropped a ten-dollar bill on the counter, picked up her order and said, "You know, I did some research myself. That large a dose is probably why it only took her hours to die, instead of days." Murdoch gave Harriet a smile. "Thanks Harriet. See you around Larissa."

"Yeah. See you around."

Murdoch was gone and Harriet was studying me as I finished my tea. Finally, I looked at her and demanded, "What?"

Shaking her head in disbelief, she said, "Hmm. You know what. When are you going to deal with this Murdoch issue?"

"That's a damn good question." I smiled. "When I have an answer, I'll let you know."

# About The Author

A native Floridian, Darlene has moved away multiple times, only to be drawn back by the smell of the sea, the sun, and the feel of sand between her toes. She and her spouse live near Darlene's hometown of Daytona Beach.

At the time of this writing, they have one rescue cat named Keke. She's part Russian Blue and quite often Darlene believes the cat is channeling a dog. Keke loves to follow her around and sit on the floor near her chair while she writes.

# OTHER BOOKS IN THIS SERIES

## A New Beginning in Coventry Beach
### A Larissa Carpenter Mystery #1

Larissa Carpenter is the one of the richest women in the country. Eighteen months ago, her spouse, Rachel, died of a brain aneurysm. Looking for a new beginning, she travels to the small town of Coventry Beach and moves into the house she and Rachel bought just before Rachel died.

Using the name Laurel Carpenito to avoid the notoriety that came with winning the largest lottery jackpot in the state's history, she begins to clear her head and think about the future.

Finding the body of a young woman she'd met only 12 hours earlier wasn't part of the future Larissa/Laurel envisioned. As if being a person of interest in one murder wasn't bad enough, she witnesses a woman stab a man on the beach in front of her house.

At the local tea and coffee shop, My Place, Laurel runs into an old high school classmate who, unknown to Larissa/Laurel, is now an FBI agent.

The owner of My Place, Harriet Walsh, has spent two years running from an ex-fiancé turned stalker. Thinking he's lost her trail, she has settled down in Coventry Beach. She and Laurel have become friends, and when Harriet disappears, Det. Murdoch is unhappy with Laurel's hiring of a search and rescue team to help find Harriet.

Will Larissa find a new beginning in Coventry Beach, or will this be just another dip in the roller-coaster ride that her life has become?

# Lust & Distrust
## A Larissa Carpenter Mystery #2

Since moving to Coventry Beach, Larissa Carpenter hasn't found life in the small beach town to provide the tranquility she expected. Not wanting everyone in town to know that she's the Larissa Carpenter who won one of the state's largest lottery jackpots, she goes by Laurel
Carpenito or LC.

Being a person of interest in two murder cases, one of which still hasn't been solved, is most unsettling and it's not the only unsettling thing in LC's life. Her attraction to Detective Angela Murdoch and the feeling that she's being followed are the other disconcerting                                            issues.

Unsure of who's following her, LC wonders if her former high school classmate, FBI Special Agent Amber Hoffner has something to do
with                                                                                    it.

Does the FBI think she's involved in the human trafficking ring? Does Detective Murdoch think she killed Natalie Kramer? Is Detective Murdoch attracted to her or is that a figment of her imagination?

Is LC right about being followed? If so, who is it? The FBI? The local police? Someone else?

# OTHER BOOKS BY THIS AUTHOR

## The Legend of Erin Foster

The Order for Morality and Justice has grown its power base and now reaches to the highest level of government. Virtually all civil rights laws are gone. The federal government is on the verge of declaring martial law nationwide.

Warrants are issued daily for the arrest of enemies of the state. When they come for Erin Foster and her partner of seven years, Alice, the Peacekeeper of The Order for Morality and Justice shoots out the front door lock. His bullet ricochets and kills Alice.

Alice's death flips a switch in Erin Foster and her mission to destroy The Order and its leader, The Reverend James Calton III, begins. In her eyes, you're either part of the solution or you're part of the problem.

# Life Is Full of Surprises

What do industrial espionage, an unsolved hit and run and a bloody knife in an ice cream carton have in common? They're all elements in the romantic mystery Life Is Full of Surprises.

Barbara Orlock and Judy Langdon have both sworn off falling in love. They agree their relationship will be no strings attached, just fun and games.

Judy's ex-lover, Carol Engram, is found dead in Judy's apartment. Actin on an anonymous tip police search Barbara's freezer and find the murder weapon, a bloody knife, hidden in an ice cream carton.

Will Barbara's faith in her business associate, Gerald, be her undoing? Was the death of Barbara's previous lover, Linda, really an accident? Who has the most to gain by Carol's death? Or maybe the question should be who has the most to gain if Barbara is convicted of Carol's murder? Can Judy unravel the mystery and clear Barbara of murder?

# The Origin of Deanna Dorak
## Nedamla Book #1

Is she merely a freak of nature…or is she from another world?

Deanna Dorak suddenly finds herself alone in the world and begins to realize that it may not even be her world. With confusing images forcing their way into her consciousness she struggles to understand who she is and why she's here. She elicits the help of her best friend and former lover, Kate, who believes that all of Deanna's problems stem from her inability to accept her mother's death. That is until she sees the gills that have begun to form on Deanna's sides. Kate brings Deanna to Dr. Jason Alexander, who vows to help her and protect her from government scientists.

Soon after, Kate's body is pulled from the river – someone broke her neck.

A frantic search for answers takes Deanna on the quest of her life. Is she the reason her friend was killed? Is Jason friend or foe? Is he holding her captive for his own scientific research? Is she really from another planet, an underwater world inhabited only by women? Can she trust the detective assigned to solve Kate's murder? Can she trust herself?

# Aneesha's Prophecy
## Nedamla Book #2

*"The daughter will return and avenge the death of her mother and those innocents killed here today."*

Dorak Deanna has come home to claim her birthright. Home, to a planet she remembers only through the implanted memories of her mother, Miktra. Home to a planet still occupied by the same Empyrean forces that forced her departure nearly thirty years ago.

The Day of Ascension is fast approaching and the Empyrean Governor of Nedamla grows more fearful of Aneesha's Prophecy with each passing day. Especially since each day seems to bring another unexplained, violent death of at least one of his soldiers. Yet the Empyror refuses his requests for more troops, assuring him that since Aneesha's child was killed during the invasion, there is no heir to ascend to the throne.

By accident Deanna discovers she has the ability to communicate, with at least one Nedamlan, by using only her thoughts. Is it possible that there are others among her people with this ability? Perhaps it will be the secret weapon she needs.

Even with the ability to mind-talk, how can one woman turn a population of women, known for their pacifism, into warriors? And if she and her warriors take Nedamla from the troops now occupying her, how will they maintain their freedom? The Empyror has more than enough troops to simply send another invasion force.

As if fighting the Empyre weren't enough to worry about, Deanna has another problem – she has fallen in love.

Will Deanna fulfill Aneesha's Prophecy? Can she return her people to a time when they were fierce warriors, asking no quarter and giving none? Will Jorsta agree to join with her?

www.ingramcontent.com/pod-product-compliance
Lightning Source LLC
Chambersburg PA
CBHW060939180626
46817CB00004B/1631